Backdraft

Shana Gray

To all the emergency services front line, and behind the scenes teams. It's a tough role. Be safe out there.

Chapter One

Did I have to prove myself again? Prove that as the new fire investigator for the regional fire marshal's office, I had the chops? After seven years, I should expect it. A woman treading into what was solely a man's world, especially new to the region, required paying some dues.

I get it.

But it would be nice if the confrontations could wait until after the scene is cleared? All I wanted to do right now was my job.

I inched forward, my helmet light piercing through the gloom of ash and smoke. This was a fatal fire, and we had to recover the victims, a mom and her kids.

My breath whooshed inside the Versa flow PPE helmet. I looked around, making sure I wasn't straying off the safe path through the gutted house. Hot spots still flared up in the walls. I'd given orders to the truck crews to keep on top of them. Every now and then, water came through the burnt-out walls like a waterfall. I was used to it, but the forensic officer just behind me wasn't. He kept shouting to turn around. I indicated it was okay, to stay on task and follow me.

We were on the second floor of an older home and had to be laddered up for a window entry. Part of the floor on the left side of the house was gone and had taken the stairs with it.

When kids were involved, everyone was tense, on edge, and desperate to locate the victims. I was too, but it was important to keep the team calm and go by the book.

Only this wasn't a rescue. It was a recovery.

I inched forward. Casting my flashlight about, looking for any indication of a body. I went deeper into the house, carefully avoiding a hole in the floor. The tension coming off the forensic officer was tangible. It irritated me, and I grit my teeth.

I heard a scratching, and I stopped, shining the flashlight around to see what could be making the noise. But there was nothing.

A tap on my shoulder startled me, but I forced myself to keep my reaction as minimal as possible. I refused to show any sign of weakness and faced the forensic officer with a blank expression.

"What's up?" I looked into his eyes. I didn't know his name yet. I assumed he'd also heard the noise.

"It's nothing." I shook my head.

"But I hear something," he yelled. There was really no need to yell, and it was further indication of his state of mind.

I patted him on the shoulder. "If you can't be in here without freaking out, then leave. I've got to find these bodies."

It was as if saying "bodies" snapped sense into him. He nodded, and his flashlight shimmered through the haze.

"Stay with me!" I called to him. It wouldn't do for him to get lost in the house. I had the floorplan imprinted in my brain. I knew where we could step, and where we couldn't. I knew which bedroom was where, and who was supposed to be in each room.

I heard scratching again. There was something in the walls. Maybe a rat trying to get out, or a bird. I couldn't get sentimental over an animal that could be harmed by the fire. I didn't like animals being hurt, but right now, we had to focus on the occupants of the house.

Something caught my eye through the doorway as some of the smoke cleared. Then it was gone as another wave of smoke and water rained down on us.

"Hey," I yelled, and the officer looked up from sifting through a pile of charred furniture that was still smoldering.

I pointed. He nodded. "Through there."

We inched our way forward. The scratching continued behind us, and the hair on the back of my neck stood up.

Stop it. Don't let your mind run away with you. This isn't your first time.

Something caught my eye, and the beam of my torch-light illuminated a pale object protruding from the ash and debris.

I knew what it was before I got close enough to confirm.

I put out my right hand to stop him. Our eyes met, and I knew by the expression on his face that he saw what I had. He glanced to the ground, his mouth moving as if he was saying something. Perhaps a prayer?

I stepped around a broken and burned door into the charred hall. I kneeled, careful not to disturb anything, and rested for the briefest moment, looking down at the small skeletal hand that reached out of a pile of burnt-up fabric.

We'd found the toddler.

I pulled the radio from my pocket, spoke into the mic to advise the team of our discovery. I took photos to document the find before marking the location and moving on down the hall.

This was going to be a long recovery.

Moving carefully through the upstairs hall toward the other bedroom, I both hoped and dreaded finding the remains of the mother and the other child.

* * *

Hours later, I needed a break. I was hot and felt a bit faint. The last thing I wanted was to pass out or puke in front of the new crew. I'd fight through pretty much any discomfort before letting them think I couldn't handle my job.

There was time for a short break before I had to get back into the building. I had to call in Shannon. She was a forensic anthropologist and needed to be on scene when a body was disarticulated. The other toddler was found in the closet, and it was clear Shannon needed to come in.

My truck was parked just the other side of the fire trucks and the police cruisers. Normally, there was room for me to pull up in front of the building, which I preferred. I've had items stolen from my truck in the past, so I liked to keep it close. I pulled off my PPE gear and Tyvek suit. I wish I'd worn my cooling vest today. Using my supply of wet wipes, I quickly washed my face and hands and then set up my cooling chair in the shade of the truck and filled the arms with ice from my big cooler.

Finally, I plopped into the chair, and it was heaven. I sat there with my arms immersed in the melting ice, legs spread out in front of me and closed my eyes. A lovely chill pushed the heat in me out. I could stay here forever. Instead, I gave myself a few more moments before getting the lunch and drinks I'd packed in the cooler. I was parched, and the ice-cold water with a drop of lime cordial hit the spot.

I kept an eye on the house and the fire crews.

It was my scene, and nobody was allowed back in the house until I said. Sure, there was a lot of power that came with my position. And yes, I'd got a lot of resistance in the beginning. But not so much anymore.

Now, they looked to me for answers, and many of the fire fighters were interested in my work. It was rewarding to be able to educate them in any small way.

Gradually, my expertise had become respected, and it wasn't as difficult to maintain a scene now. This was the first fire I was working in this region. I wasn't supposed to begin the new role until Monday, but I'd been called in early for this.

I was glad I'd decided to arrive a couple days early to scope out Oak Creek. My household items and vehicle were being shipped. It wasn't so bad staying in a hotel. My bed got made and the room was cleaned. There was something to be said about not having to do it myself.

I watched my new crew. They didn't know what to expect from me, unless they'd heard things through the pipeline. I knew I was tough, but I also knew I had compassion. For both the victims and the crews that were on scene.

For this fire, I was definitely going to suggest to the chief that they call in some emotional support. Whenever there's kids involved... I sighed.

What a way to start my first day.

I paired up a grape, a chunk of cheese, and a Ritz cracker. After munching on them and swigging water, I began to feel a bit more human. Cooling down, filling my belly, and rehydrating did wonders for a girl.

I checked my watch. I still had about forty-five minutes before Shannon would be here. I'd catch up on some notes.

I reached over for my clipboard and jabbed my finger on the edge of the aluminum cover, my nail getting caught in the seam.

"Shit." I pulled my nail out, and the tip had a chip in it I'd have to file, then find a spa to fix it.

I indulged in pretty nails and pretty lingerie. I had to keep my feminine side somehow in this male-dominated world.

Taylor pulled up to the site and maneuvered his way between the emergency vehicles. Driving the coroner van had its perks and gave him quick access to the scene. He wanted to find a spot fairly close to the house. He dreaded calls like this. It was bad enough when anyone died in a fire, but when there were kids involved...

Weaving his way through the parked vehicles, he eased to a halt before the fire hose that ran across the street. He took out his notebook, making a notation of the time, the weather conditions, and the temperature. All that was important when doing the postmortem and cause of death.

He knew most of the fire crews quite well. He'd been called to a lot of scenes, not just fire, but accidents, suspicious deaths and the like. He also went out drinking with them on occasion, even if they had to twist his arm a little. Taylor didn't mind going to Kali's. Just not every day. Playing football with the crews was a highlight of working with them, and it gave him the release he needed sometimes. So they all knew each other both professionally and privately.

He got out and walked over to the crowd by the

pumper. It was a quiet scene today. The hush was palpable. Taylor clenched his jaw, knowing what he was about to face.

"Hey, Chief," he greeted Ralph Gregory, affectionately known as Rage not because he raged, but because of the way he bellowed his orders so everyone could hear him. He was in command of the scene today.

"Doc." Rage reached out and took Taylor's hand, shaking his head. "Not a good day."

He agreed with him and looked around at the faces of the other firefighters. They were all solemn, and he didn't blame them one little bit.

"So where's the new investigator?"

"She's over there." He nodded.

Taylor looked over at the truck. "She? I didn't know the new fire investigator was a woman." He'd only ever met one at a conference a couple of years ago in Denver. Taylor smiled at the memory. She'd certainly been good at igniting a fire.

"Yeah, she's new to our region, but she knows her stuff. Her reputation preceded her. She's tough, accurate, and she took control of the scene right away." Rage smiled at Taylor.

"Whatever makes this scene safe and properly investigated," Taylor told him, knowing the chief was baiting him. But he wouldn't bite.

"Yes, she's waiting for you and the forensic anthropologist. Found three bodies. One is disarticulated, the other two haven't been recovered yet. Waiting for both you and the anthropologist."

Taylor nodded and touched his fingertips to his eyebrows. "Gotcha. I'll get suited up.

At his van, Taylor pulled on his Tyvek suit and PPE. It was a hot day and wouldn't be long until he was sweating.

He walked over to the house and stood in the shade in front of the white picket fence that ringed the yard.

He gazed up at the ruined structure. He was dreading going in this time and drew in a deep breath, glad for the shade of the tree. He glanced back and saw the investigator walking toward him. He couldn't see her face behind the mask, so he just lifted a hand in acknowledgment. She did the same. She indicated for him to follow her, and he did as he was told.

When she led him over to the ladder truck, he knew that they were not going in through the front door. He watched her climb the rungs and followed her up the ladder. Firefighters followed behind them. She easily climbed over the sill of the burned-out window and into the gloom of the one of the upstairs bedrooms. Taylor quickly followed her, and she gave instructions on the layout so he knew where he could go and where he couldn't.

"Don't go over there," she told him and pointed.

Looks like the whole floor was gone as well as the stairs to the main floor.

Taylor flicked on his helmet light and followed the beam as well as the investigator.

He saw where the first body was. It was marked with a cone.

He met her eyes, and she nodded. Taylor sucked in a breath and crouched down. May as well get on with it.

She knelt next to him and gently swished some of the ash away with a brush until more of the child was exposed.

She took photos, and he stared at the body. Sometimes being the coroner was worse than being an ER doc.

. . .

Taylor checked the other two bodies. He wouldn't be the one extracting them from the scene. It would be the fire investigator and the forensic archaeologist in a time-consuming retrieval. They were buried under the layers of ash and debris from the house that had come down.

There were still hot spots smoldering in the walls, and he was anxious to get out of the building. He didn't know how firefighters did it. For him, coming into a scene like this took a lot of steel. They were trained for it, and it sometimes seemed like a lot of them lusted for it.

What kind of person wanted to be a fire investigator? Coming in after the fact. Looking for bodies, for the fire's origin and cause. He peered through the ash and smoke hanging on the air. All he saw were charred outlines of what had once been someone's home. A home that had engulfed a mom and her two children.

The aftermath of the fire and water was incredible, and Taylor marveled that anyone could make sense of it.

After inspecting the bodies as best he could under these conditions, he indicated he was done. She turned, and he followed her back down the hall. She paused as they entered the original room they'd climbed into. She tilted her head as if she was listening for something.

He listened and frowned, not hearing a thing and pretty sure he didn't want to either, if he was honest. Taylor wasn't freaked or nervous, just eager to get out of the house. Knocking down a fire and running into a fully engulfed burning building was beyond his scope of comprehension. But then not everyone could pronounce death and perform autopsies.

The investigator tapped him on the shoulder. He looked into her mask and goggles to see if he could recognize her. The gloom in the room shrouded her face, and the light on her helmet blinded him. She yelled loud enough loud enough for him to hear.

"You go on. Something I need to check."

"You want me to stay with you?" He felt he should hang back with her in case something happened.

He could see her cheeks bunch up the bridge of her nose, and the corner of her eyes crinkled. He realized she must be grinning under her mask.

She shook her head. "No, I'm fine. You go." She waved her hand toward the window.

"Okay." Taylor picked his way back, doing his best to take the same steps they'd made on the way in. He glanced over his shoulder and saw she was touching the wall just inside the bedroom door. Was there a fire behind it? He climbed through the window and braced himself on the top rung of the ladder. The outline of her body bled into the gloom, and the light on her helmet haloed around her. She held a piece of equipment, raised it, and then swung it into the charred and burned drywall. She continued to break up the wall.

He was impressed at her lack of hesitation and tenacity.

At the bottom of the ladder, he pulled off his mask and hood.

"She's up there alone. Swinging something at the wall. She looks like she has it handled," he advised the crew.

"She'll be okay," the lieutenant told him.

"It looks like she's trying to pull down the wall," he said, and took off his gloves, balling them up.

The three men looked up at the window. Taylor saw a shadow of concern on the lieutenant's face. Maybe he should've waited.

She stuck her head out the window and waved her hand.

"Move the ladder closer. She's holding something."

Taylor stepped back and unzipped his Tyvek suit. It was damn hot, but he didn't look away from her. Had they missed a body?

He watched her climb out the window with ease and make it down the ladder. At the bottom, the firefighters surrounded her. She did have something in her arms.

Taylor hung back and watched, curious to see what she'd found.

News crews were on scene, and he wasn't surprised. This would be a huge headline in their next edition and was probably online already.

One of reporters pointed in the direction of the huddle around the investigator. The rest turned like a pack and crowded in to see what was happening.

They blocked his view and were just as curious to see what she'd brought out of the burned-up house.

Chapter Two

I smashed the Halligan into the wall and yanked down the crumbling drywall. I kept at it until I had a hole big enough to look inside. There were no telltale signs of fire in the wall.

I had no idea what to expect, but the scratching was driving me crazy. It was probably just a mouse, a rat, or even a bird, but I couldn't just ignore the sound. I looked into the hole, and the light on my helmet illuminated the gloom and darkness. A low growl greeted me, and I froze.

I half expected the unseen creature to leap at me as it tried to beat a hasty escape. I leaned in a little more and peered down. At first, I couldn't see anything and moved my head so the helmet light pierced into the far corners.

Even though I was somewhat prepared, I was still startled when two glowing eyes stared back at me. I gasped and retreated quickly. Scratching continued, and there was a sad little mewling sound.

"Don't be such a baby," I told myself and peeked in again. Two big green eyes looked back at me.

It was a cat. A black cat. Either that, or he was covered in soot and smoke.

"Oh hey, little guy. It's all okay."

I grabbed the kitty and tucked him under my arm. I leaned out the window and waved my arm indicating I was ready to come down, then picked up the Halligan propped against the wall.

Juggling the cat, Halligan, and holding the ladder, it wasn't easy climbing down. Thankfully the cat was relatively still, but I hung on to him tight. I had to descend effortlessly, like I'd been born to do it because I could feel all the eyes below watching me.

Finally, back on the driveway I let out a breath and gave the cat a pat on the head rubbing him gently. He was black underneath all the muck and wet fur.

The crew gathered around to see him.

"So, there was something in the wall," the forensic officer commented.

I nodded. "The scratching was driving me nuts, and I had to see what was doing it. Poor little guy. He's lucky he didn't get toasted. The baseboard was missing, and I guess he climbed up the wall cavity."

"He sure is a mess," another said and gave me a wet towel to clean him up

I wrapped him in the towel. "I'll take him back to my truck. Hopefully, he'll settle. Thanks."

When I emerged from the barrier of firefighters, a barrage of questions was thrown at me from photographers.

"Is that a cat?"

"Where did you find the cat?"

"What are you going to do with the cat?"

The questions kept coming and they were all about the

cat, nothing about the victims. I was glad too, because the last thing I wanted to do was discuss the deceased. Not only was it upsetting to me, the crew and family members, it wasn't something to talk about to the media. You had to be careful with them around. They had boom mics and could hear the slightest whisper. I never said anything of significance until I was in a secure environment.

I gave interviews if necessary, but I was always cautious on the info I provided. Never more than necessary, just enough to ease the questions, and nothing to compromise the case.

Not today though. I wasn't prepared to answer them and pushed my way through the crowd.

A house had caught fire, and three victims died inside, a mother and her children. It was tragic and all these reporters cared about was a cat? Some of the firefighters stepped between me and the reporters so I could escape the crush behind the closest rig.

Chief Gregory was putting his radio on the fender of the truck. "What you got there?"

"I heard something in the walls. It was this sad little guy. You don't have a box or anything that I can put him in, do you?" I asked as I checked the cat over.

Chief Gregory gave him a stroke and shook his head. "No, I got nothing. Sorry about that. Why don't we give him a bit of a cleanup?"

Over the next few minutes, the two of us cleaned up the cat so it wasn't such a filthy ball of fur. He let us handle him like he knew we were helping.

This gave me a new insight to the Chief. He had a soft side and wasn't all ragey like his nick name suggested. I didn't know why they called him Rage, but his size, presence, and no-nonsense appearance suited perfectly. He was probably in his forties and a good-looking guy.

Not that I was interested...well, perhaps in the future once I was settled here, but not now. The last thing I needed were complications that went with a budding relationship.

Once done, I left the captain and went to my truck. We were still waiting for the coroner and Shannon. I glanced around, and there was no sign of her yet. Once she got here, we had to recover the bodies for transport to the morgue.

I wrapped Kitty in a space blanket which he wasn't overly excited about it thanks to the crinkly noise it made.

In the back of my truck I made a nest with some shirts and a blanket, opened the windows a bit and grateful the truck was in the shade. It had clouded over, and rain threatened so he should be fine. Plus, there really wasn't anything else I could do right now.

Finally, I could shed my PPE. If it was going to rain, I wanted to let it wash over me. It would cool me down and help to rinse away some of the grunge.

I wish Shannon would hurry up.

Just as I was shimmying out of my Tyvek, a male voice from behind made me pause. My arms stuck in the sleeves.

"Hey, what you got there?"

I turned to see who it was. A jolt of recognition made me lose my balance and he reached out to help steady me.

I knew him.

"Pardon?" I croaked, my mind racing. Where had I seen him before? My body reacted in a way that told me it remembered quite well.

But... who... how?

Oh my God! Denver!

From that conference trip a few years ago.

We'd scorched the sheets at that hotel. He was there for a medical conference, and I was there for a bomb and explosives seminar.

I kept my cool and did my best to remain professional. He did the same. But, the smile that curved his lips was exactly how he'd looked at me in Denver. One side of his oh, so kissable mouth turned up in a sexy grin and his eyes, those deep, sea blue eyes had cast me adrift years ago, almost did the same now.

He remembered too.

"Ah, there was a cat in the wall." I looked at him and realized I was still standing with my arms trapped in the suit. He must have noticed too. He raised his eyebrows. Was he remembering how he'd used his silk tie to bind me while...

Nope, I couldn't let my mind run to the erotic, but damn, it would be so easy to. I quickly shed the suit, kicked my feet out and reached down to ball it up. I always wore a tank top and shorts under the suit to help keep my temperature down, but under that was some very sexy lingerie.

It didn't do me any favors now. His steamy expression heated me up, and I tried not to remember our sexually uninhibited and wild weekend. But, those memories came rushing back nearly stealing my breath away.

The way he watched me remove my suit threw me back to the hotel room. The room where I stripped for him. The room where we discovered each other. The room where we agreed it was just for the weekend.

No strings.

No commitment.

No exchange of contact info.

And it had been mind blowing.

I drew in a ragged breath and smoothed my top and shorts. I kept my eyes on the group when I shook out my hair and tied it back up in a high pony. It was damp with sweat, and curls slipped out of the clip.

"What are you doing here?" I was finally able to form words, and my voice was harsher than I'd meant it to be. This distraction and reminder of - *that weekend* - wasn't what I needed right now! Nothing could interfere with this new position or jeopardize my reputation.

"You just took me in there? Didn't you recognize me?" He pointed at the house.

I shook my head. "No, I didn't. We were head to toe in protective gear." I furrowed my brows and continued, "I mean, what are you doing here?"

"I'm the medical examiner," he told me and crossed his bare, very muscled arms over his equally muscled chest.

"Medical examiner? You're a doctor." I was confused.

"I am a doctor." He stiffened, and a tight expression crossed his face. I guess I struck a nerve.

"Yes, I know, but a doctor doctor. You know..." I waved my hand, feeling impatient I had to explain.

"No I don't know." His reply was clipped, and his expression told me I'd said something terribly wrong. "I *am* a doctor."

"I know that, but the last time we—

I trailed off, because if I brought that up, it would also bring our past slamming right into the present. I wasn't sure I was ready for that. It would be complicated enough to maneuver through this potential minefield.

I glanced around to see if anyone was watching. Thankfully, no one was. The last thing I needed today, on the first day of a new job, were memories of our wild and uninhibited sexy weekend.

"Well, the last time we saw each other, you were a doctor and not the coroner."

"Career change." He stepped back and put his hands on his hips, emphasizing the strength and power of his body. A ripple of desire caught me unaware, and I bit back a gasp.

Time to get back to business.

"Okay, let's, uh, move on. Shall we?" I didn't mean to sound edgy again, but I knew I did. "We have three bodies in there for removal. The one in the closet is going to be the most challenging."

He nodded. "Yes, I expect you've called for the forensic anthropologist?"

I nodded. "She should be here soon, and once recovery is done, the bodies will be sent to your morgue."

"You'll be there too?" he asked.

My heart did a double beat. "Of course. I'm always at the postmortems."

"Great. I'll have the assistant let you know when we've got the PM scheduled."

"Perfect, thanks," I replied.

Our eyes met, and I was pretty sure he was thinking the same thing I was.

It was going to be a long day.

* * *

Taylor was gone by the time Shannon arrived. He may have left, but I was still wound tighter than a drum. I couldn't shake it, and Shannon knew me well enough to pick up on it. We'd known each other for years. When I'd started training, she was also sitting in on a course, and we connected quickly. We'd shared some fun times together during the course and did a few girls weekends away after. We kept in touch over the years and had the occasional fatal scene where we crossed over. Aside from the scene, it was great to see each other in person. But I had to be cautious. I'd never told her about the weekend.

I never told anyone.

She was the one that had told me about this opportunity. I was glad to have her by my side as we crawled through the debris to recover the bodies. It definitely was not a nice task.

I briefed her on the three bodies, and she was in pure professional business mode. That's how Shannon was. She was all business when it came to fires, but once the workday was done, she turned into a wild thing. We'd had lots of fun together, and she brought out my less-inhibited side. Much like Taylor had. We'd gotten ourselves into some fun situations.

Shannon drew in a breath. "Okay, so one is beneath debris with only a hand exposed. That's the toddler. The child is in a closet in the second bedroom and is disarticulated. The mom is in the third bedroom."

"That's right."

She shook her head. "So sad. Is there any other family?"

"I'm not sure. I haven't been informed yet."

"What do you think? Suspicious or accidental?"

"I haven't done a full investigation yet, but so far, not suspicious. Depends what I find on the main floor. Let's gear up so we can get in there."

Inside the house, I put my toolkit, which looked much like a tackle box, down where we'd be working to recover the first body

Shannon crouched down in front of the closet. She always whispered a few words quiet words to the bodies. I never asked her what she said. I respected her moment.

She took out the tools — a trowel, brushes of different sizes, and some other items she used to gently move away the debris to expose the body. It was much like peeling back an onion layer by layer, and as the body was revealed, we were able to remove it all. The recovery would be time-consuming, and this was the first body.

I held out a piece of aluminum foil, and Shannon carefully placed the bones and flesh she retrieved on the sheet. I layered another on top and gently pressed the foil together. It molded around the bones and kept them intact to transport for Shannon's examination later. It was especially important for the numerous bones of the hands and feet. I marked the tin foil with black marker stating the location it was found, left leg, right arm, etc...

All evidence was bagged, labeled, and photographed.

Hours later, the bodies had been removed. The evidence bags had been sealed and documented with chain of custody tags and placed in the coroner's van. The bodies would be taken to the morgue for autopsy the next day.

I would wait for a time notification since I was always at the PMs. Tomorrow, with us all in attendance for documentation, the evidence seals would be broken, and the autopsy would begin.

After the hours of work, I'd completely forgotten about Taylor. Now, with a moment to think, I was surprised when a tremor of excitement at seeing him tomorrow shivered along my flesh. But on the heels of that, I remembered the cat in my truck.

"Shit!"

"What? What's wrong?" Shannon asked in the middle of removing her protective gear and flung her arms out. She was always easily startled and ready to bolt if needed.

She made me laugh. It's so easy to jump scare her. Not that I did it on purpose or anything.

I laughed. "Calm down. Nothing crazy. I found a cat in the wall earlier and put him in my truck."

She grimaced. "Arg, you could have a nasty-smelling truck waiting for you."

I close my eyes briefly and shake my head. "Probably, but it's just par for the course right now. Anyway, the poor little guy was distraught, and I wasn't going to just let him fend for himself."

"Once you check on him and we get cleaned up, we need to chill and relax. It was an awful long day, and I'm hungry, parched and getting moody."

"You're always hungry and parched. But, rarely moody." I smiled as I shed my own gear.

"What can I say, I love food. And how do you think I achieved my wonderfully curvy body?" She ran her hands down her sides and over her shapely hips. "By starving myself? Nope. By enjoying life, love, food, and my body."

"I think you look fabulous," I told her. She wasn't as tall as me, and her curves couldn't be hidden in any type of clothing or workwear. She exuded a sexuality that must come off her in waves of pheromones, because guys flocked to her.

"Thank you. And I am happy to oblige on the food and drink front." She gave me a saucy smile, and I knew what she had in mind.

Bar time, patio time, shots, and who knew what food she would order. It depended on where we went, but the table usually groaned, that I knew for sure. And we'd unashamedly ate it all.

"You know what, I would love to be your partner in

crime right now, but I can barely keep my eyes open, I stink, I have to pee, and I've got that damn cat to deal with."

"I. Am. Shocked. What happened to you? You used to be fun." She planted her hands on her hips and gave me the stare.

I could have taken offense, but I was too tired. She was right.

I lifted a shoulder. "I don't know. My spark is gone. I've been focused so much on work and the move."

She nodded. "Girlfriend, you need to party and," she looked around, "get laid. There's plenty to choose from right here. Check out that Chief over there. Yummy." She waggled her eyebrows.

It felt good to laugh again. It seemed like ages since I had. "Not your kinda party, my dear. I could use time to relax though, and okay, I will admit I could use a few drinks. But I gotta deal with things first. You got my number, right?"

She nodded.

"Okay, then let me see what I can work out and call me in a few hours. I checked my watch and groaned. "It's one a.m. Nothing will be open now, and I really need some sleep. Dinner later?

She wagged her finger at me. "Fine, dinner later. When's the PM?"

"It's tomorrow, or is that today? I don't know. I'll probably hear in the morning."

"Okay, I'll see you at the PM anyway, but don't you dare think you're going to bail on our girls' night."

"Okay, okay. By then I'll probably feel more human. We can sort it tomorrow?" I raised my eyebrows and nodded.

"Today," Shannon said and smiled.

I rubbed my eyes. "Yes, yes, today. Actually, I like the idea of us going out. Now I need to check on that cat."

I opened the truck, fully expecting a howling cat to launch itself at me, but it was silent. Maybe he was asleep. I moved the nest I'd made earlier.

"He's not here." I sniffed cautiously. "There's no kitty aroma emanating from the truck either. He's gone." I looked at Shannon.

"Well, where'd he go?" she asked.

Chapter Three

I didn't expect the cat to cause this much trouble right off the hop. I don't see how he got out of the vehicle without some help.

I glanced around, and it was then I noticed a piece of paper tucked under the windshield wiper. Plucking it from underneath the rubber holding it down, I opened it up to read.

I took your cat. Didn't seem right to leave it in the truck. Shame on you. It is at Wags + Whiskers. If you don't claim within twenty-four hours, I'm taking him.

I stared at the words. There was no signature or name, and I grit my teeth. That was pretty ballsy. Who did this person think they were?

I drew in a breath and splayed my fingers, a habit I'd developed years ago when stressed. It helped me to ground myself. Even my mood ring indicated I was upset.

The cat being taken to Wags & Whiskers was a good thing. Even if it was a little out of the ordinary for someone to take it upon themselves to do it.

I glanced around and was relieved nothing else appeared to be missing. Just the cat. I'd find out Wags & Whiskers contact info and give them a call. Maybe they could keep the kitty for a few days until I got settled.

It could be a blessing in disguise really, a safe place for the cat until I found a home for him. Or I decided to keep him.

I froze. Where did that thought come from? I'd never wanted a cat before. My life was too fluid. I couldn't keep a cat in my line of work—even if they were pretty self-sufficient.

Sometimes, I'd be gone for days.

I shook my head. No way could I take the kitty home. As the words crossed my mind, a tinge of regret pinched my heart.

"What's up?" Shannon asked. "You were a million miles away just now."

"Just thinking about the cat and what to do with him," I told her while folding up the towels and jacket that had been his little nest.

"What do you mean? You should keep him. He's homeless now." Alarm ringed her voice, and I met her gaze. She was an utter softie when it came to animals.

"I know, but how can I keep a cat? Who'll take care of him when I'm away?"

She nodded and looked glum. "Good point."

On the upside, I forced myself to relax, knowing the cat was safe at the kitty spa and I had twenty-four hours to decide what to do before I contacted Wags & Whiskers.

Shannon had packed her things and was loading up

her vehicle. I was doing the same, only the face of the furry little munchkin kept popping up in my mind's eye. He had given me some seriously sad eyes when I first rescued him.

My job here was done, at least for now, unless something else cropped up. After giving Shannon a hug goodbye, I went over to Rage and the rest of his crew. They were also packing up.

"You guys were great." I shook their hands. "Thank you. It's been a very long day...night...whatever. I'm pretty sure everyone is ready to get back to the firehouse." I paused, passing my gaze over their faces. "This was a tough one. The captain and I will arrange for someone to come to the firehouse to speak to you if needed. Kids are always tough. Don't hesitate to take the help offered. There's no shame in it."

I looked at the crew in front of me. Some stared at the ground and others watched me. I nodded at them, hoping the words would encourage them to seek whatever emotional support they needed.

"How's your cat?" one of the fire crew asked.

"Well, that's a helluva thing. The cat's gone. Someone took it and left a note on my windshield." I held up the piece of paper and waved it. Apparently, I can find this cat at Wags & Whiskers. Any of you know where that is?"

For the first time since I came on scene, they laughed. The mood lightened, and I wondered what was so funny."

"Ah, Mel's place. She's a pet groomer and lives on the other side of town. Your cat will be in safe hands with her."

"Well, he's hardly my cat," I corrected.

"Didn't look like that to me." A female firefighter smiled at me. "I guess you took ownership when you put it in your truck."

"Okay, okay. Maybe he is kind of my cat. But I've been given a timeline on retrieving him."

"I didn't see anyone going to your truck, and shouldn't it have been locked?" Rage raised his eyebrows.

It should've been locked. "Yes, I usually do. I shall endeavor to do better."

"Good," he said and gave me a small smile before commanding the attention of his crew. "We're going to wrap it up here and be on our way." He turned to me. "Do you have somewhere to stay tonight?"

"Yes, I'll be staying at a hotel for a while until I can find a place." I wasn't going to mention that this position and location was a trial run. The hotel was my safety net. If I didn't feel like this was the place for me, I would have less ties to cut in order to move on.

"Some of us are heading to Kali's for breakfast. This is our last twenty-four, and we're off for four. Feel free to join us if you like."

"Thanks, I appreciate the invitation." While part of me wanted to jump in with both feet and spend some time with the crew here, I was too wiped to even think about it.

We said our goodbyes, and I shuffled over and climbed into the driver's seat of my truck. Pressing my head on the seat back, I drew in a deep breath. I couldn't remember the last time I peed, and just like that, I needed to find a restroom in a hurry. I wheeled the vehicle out and made it made to my hotel room before I burst.

Relief.

I craved a shower and turned on the water to its hottest setting. Eager to get the soiled clothes off, I stripped leaving everything in a pile on the floor.

Steam filled the bathroom, and I stepped under the steaming water. The smell of the fire came off me in rivers and scented the clouds of steam. I wrinkled my nose in distaste. The stench of a fire scene always turned my stomach.

I soaped myself and washed my hair to get every trace of the smell off. My hair was so thick that I usually had to thin it out in order to manage it. It needed a trim as well, so it was a job to clean.

It took three shampoos, a rinse with vinegar and then conditioner to get the smell out. Finally, all I could smell was green apples. I stood under the rain shower watching the suds and bubbles, no longer gray with soot and grime, swirl down the drain.

My back ached. My knees were tender. My shoulders complained. Hours of being on my hands and knees beside Shannon had taken its toll.

I placed my hands on the tiled wall and leaned forward. The hot water slid over my shoulders and down my back, and it was glorious. I could stay like this forever. My mind darkened, and Taylor's face etched against the inside of my eyelids. I wondered what he was doing and allowed a memory in.

I imagined his hands on me and moaned. My exhausted body obviously wasn't too tired for arousal.

Sexual heat, seductive, sultry.

I jolted when my hands slipped. I'd gone too deep into my dream.

The ache for Taylor was still strong, and I turned off the tap and swept the water out of my eyes. I grabbed a towel and wound my hair in it, then quickly dried myself. I was hungry and I was thirsty. I remembered the invite to break-fast, but I just couldn't do it. I was shattered. Instead, I grabbed a bottle of water from my cooler and an energy bar to tide me over.

The bed looked like heaven, and I swear the white duvet and pillows beckoned me over like a siren. Pulling back the sheets, I dropped naked into the soft coziness.

The last thing I thought about was Taylor. Just what was he doing here anyways?

* * *

It was late, or early, however you wanted to look at it, when Taylor accepted the three bodies and signed the paperwork. He would let the assistant schedule and notify everyone about the PM. He was too tired to even think about it now.

Drea, as he'd called her when they met in Denver, would most likely attend. The fire investigator usually did, and she said she'd be there. He wondered how it would go. It had been a shock when he'd realized who she was, and memories of their weekend together came barreling back.

Taylor filed the paperwork and sealed the bodies into the drawer. He wondered what she was doing now. With the bodies having arrived here at the morgue at this ungodly hour, he knew she was probably done for the time being.

He hadn't forgotten their weekend in Denver. It had been the most scorching sex he'd ever had. Who knew why, but their connection was incredible. He'd even felt it again today.

Perhaps it was the lack of commitment. They'd agreed to the weekend, and it'd been damn awesome.

Nothing had compared since, and every now and then, she crossed his mind. He went into his office and took one last look at his calendar for the week. It'd been a draining day. He'd overseen a couple of autopsies and waited for the victims of the fire to arrive. Now he had to go home and sleep.

His phone pinged with a text. It was the crew from today. Mac, one of the firefighters, said they were going to Kali's for breakfast and asked if he wanted to join them.

He quickly typed back

No, thanks. I need to go home.

He wanted to ask if Drea was going to be there, but the last thing he needed to do was get tongues wagging on that front.

He closed his computer, flicked off the lights, and yawned. Yep, he needed sleep. It would be easy to just relax in his truck and snooze, but he wanted his bed. He was eager to get home.

His route home took him past the ER, where he'd spent all his time prior to switching to pathology. If there was any other way to drive from his office and not go past the ER, he would. But there wasn't, and it was forced exposure.

He didn't look at the bright light that screamed emergency, nor at the ambulances in the bay with their lights flashing. The illumination of their emergency lights reflected inside his truck, and that was as close as he wanted to be. He hadn't been back in the ER since the pandemic, nor did he want to.

Yep. It was time to just go home. But the whole drive there he couldn't get Drea out of his head.

* * *

A sound in the hall startled me. My eyes refused to open, so I just lay there, grudgingly pushing myself up through the layers of sleep.

There was no light behind my eyelids, so I wasn't sure if

it was night or day, nor did I have any idea what time it was. I was completely turned around time wise and had no desire to emerge from my comfy cocoon.

I snuggled into the duvet a little deeper, far too cozy to contemplate pushing the blankets aside. The pillows, sheets, duvet... Everything was sublimely perfect.

Maybe I could turn my phone off and simply stay here all day.

My phone buzzed, and I groaned. I didn't move until my sense of duty overtook my need for rest and sleep. Any number of things could require my attention.

I reached out for my phone on the nightstand, still refusing to move my body. If I could just reach it and pull it into the bed, I could stay here a little bit longer.

My fingers snagged on the charger cord, and I wiggled them to bring it closer. I almost had it, but it fell to the floor.

"Crap." Now I really had to move.

I rolled over and leaned out of the bed, searching for my phone.

"Gotcha." I grabbed it and nestled back in the pillows, holding it close to my face. My eyes were still prickly and refused to focus. I squinted at the message blurring the screen. Blinking away the sleepiness, I came alert in a hurry to see it was a note from the coroner's office. The autopsies were scheduled for later today.

It was only nine thirty. Thank God.

I relaxed back into the pillows with my arms flung out, phone still in my hand. I did not want to get up. Maybe I could squeeze in another couple of hours sleep, but my mind had already kicked into overdrive. The biggest question on my mind was if I'd made the right decision coming here?

It wasn't the first, nor would it be the last time I would

ask myself that. So far, the only exposure I'd had to Oak Creek and its people was yesterday at the fire scene. Other than Shannon and Taylor. I had no problem talking with the fire crews, it was a camaraderie we all seemed to have, even if we didn't know each other.

It was too early to judge if I'd made the right choice, but I was always ready to split if necessary. The urge to flee, and be able to move at the drop of a hat, was my nemesis. I wasn't entirely sure where it came from and hoped that one day I could shake it and settle down.

And seeing Taylor! What a mind fuck that was.

Then I remembered the cat.

I had to call about the cat.

My heart hurt for the little guy. I knew I couldn't keep him in the hotel, and if I wanted to keep him, I'd have to figure out where I was going to live if I stayed. Regardless, with or without him, I couldn't stay in a hotel forever.

I googled Wags & Whiskers and wasn't surprised by the whacky results. I fine-tuned the search by adding the words "pet groomer".

"Ah, there you are." I pressed the number, and a woman picked up.

"This is Mel."

"Oh, hi, Mel. My name is Andrea, and I think a black cat was brought in to you yesterday?"

"Oh, yes. He's here. What a sweetie. He's all washed up and ready to go anytime you want to come by," she said.

"Actually, I was the fire investigator that found the cat. Someone took him out of my truck and left a note saying they were taking him to you. I'm living in a hotel at the moment, so I need to make some arrangements for him. The note said I had twenty-four hours to claim him or they'd take him home, but I really don't want that, since I have no idea who they are."

"Oh, right. I didn't see the person that dropped him off, my other groomer did. I'll tell you what, we'll keep him here and tell the other person to check back in a few days if they happen to call or come by. Then we can sort this out."

I sat up in the darkened room, surprised how talking to Mel relieved my concern for the cat. I guess I wanted him after all, which meant I either had to find someplace permanent to live or not work here.

"Thank you so much. I will be in touch, here's my number." I gave it to Mel and she promised to call should anybody contact her about the cat.

I dropped the phone on the bed and stood to open the blackout draperies. Light flooded the room, momentarily blinding me until my eyes adjusted.

Oh my, the countryside was lovely. I could also see part of the town off to the right, and I wondered if Taylor lived here or elsewhere.

He was coming up in my thoughts often. It was because we'd been at the fire scene, and would see each other today again at the PM. Not because we'd spent a smoking-hot weekend together in the not-to-distant past.

My stomach grumbled its displeasure. I needed food.

I'd lost track of time and couldn't remember the last time I'd eaten. Then I remembered the cafe the firefighters had told me about. I would love a stack of pancakes and bacon.

I began to feel somewhat human after washing up, and I managed to get myself out the door in thirty minutes. I whispered a silent thank you when I saw the coffee station in the lobby. I made myself two cups of coffee, definitely needing a kick start.

"Ms. Trask?"

I turned to the registration desk. "Yes?"

"This note came for you," he said.

"Oh, thank you. I wasn't expecting anything." I looked at both sides of the envelope. My room number was scrawled on the front. "Do you know who left it?"

"No, I'm sorry. It was waiting on the concierge desk early this morning."

"Hmm, weird. Thank you."

"You're welcome."

I stuffed the envelope in my bag and juggled the two cups as I raced out of the hotel.

I gulped some coffee as I walked, careful not to spill, and moaned in delight. Boy, I needed that boost. But what I really needed were some of those amazing pancakes I'd been told about at the diner run by a woman named Kali.

Biting the edge of the open coffee cup, I wrangled all my stuff so I could unlock and open the truck door.

Inside, I wolfed down the coffee while plugging the cafe address into my GPS.

I opened the second cup and drank it while I followed the GPS's instructions. I barely noticed the drive over there and was shocked when I arrived. It was kind of freaky really, like I'd driven on autopilot. I didn't like using GPS for that reason, but I knew I'd get myself settled in after a few days.

The parking lot was full. I groaned, not really up to a crowd, but I saw one of the guys from the fire yesterday inside, so I knew there was a chance someone had spotted me, and they'd know I'd bailed on coming in.

I sat for a minute in the shady parking spot on the edge of the lot. The truck stuck out like a sore thumb, but I had no choice. My SUV, along with my minimal household items, were being shipped and should arrive in a couple of days.

Inside, I chose a seat in the corner with the window and let out a burst of air when I plopped down.

The waitress came to take my order.

"I hear you have great pancakes." I smiled up at her. She was young, and her hair was braided back from her head like the women on Vikings.

"So they say." She smiled back.

"Great, coffee with lots of cream, pancakes with a side of bacon please, oh, and extra butter."

She scribbled on the pad. "I'll be right back with your coffee."

"Thanks."

She walked away, and I scanned the cafe. The firefighter I'd recognized was leaving, and he nodded in my direction. I replied in kind.

Drawing in a contented breath, I dug out my planner and put it on the table. I flipped it open to today, skimmed the notes I'd made, and turned to a blank journal page. I tried using calendar apps, but I inevitably failed. Usually, I journaled before going to bed, but last night had been a wash. I was making notes when a tray slid in front of me piled high with pancakes, bacon, pots of butter, a big steaming mug of coffee and a pitcher of cream.

"This looks amazing. Thank you."

"You're welcome. Enjoy."

With a pencil in my left hand and a fork in the right, I continued to write and eat, and only one small drop of syrup pooled on the open page. I blotted it off. Mmm, the crew hadn't exaggerated when they'd said how good the pancakes here were.

I turned to my to do-list for the move to Oak Creek and

scanned down the page. I wasn't able to check many things off yet. I closed the planner, took a couple of big gulps of coffee and had just speared a slice of bacon when I heard a male voice.

"Good morning, how are you today?" I jumped when he slid into the seat across from me and took a sip from the coffee he had with him.

I was stunned he was so bold.

"I hope you don't mind me stopping by like this. I saw you sitting here all by yourself and thought maybe you need a good hometown welcome."

"Ah, that's nice of you, but I'm sorry, I don't know who you are?" I tended to be leery of people at first. I put my pencil down and stabbed at the pancakes as I kept an eye on him.

He set his mug on the table. "I just want to let you know that yesterday went really well. I think you did an awesome job, and I know it probably wasn't easy coming in brand-new like you did. But your reputation has preceded you, so we knew the investigation would go well."

I quickly put it together and realized what he was referring to. I pointed my fork at him. "Oh, you were on scene yesterday? I'm sorry, I didn't recognize you."

"No problem. We didn't officially meet," he said and smiled.

"Thank you. I appreciate that. It certainly wasn't the best kind of scene for a first day. But then, we can't pick and choose, can we?" He still hadn't told me his name, so I was very careful with my words.

"No, we can't. Are you heading back over there after the autopsy?"

"Yes." I wasn't about to say too much. Less is more, and

I'd learned to keep quiet while on scenes and away from them. You never knew who was listening.

Because of the fatalities, the scene was being held by Oak Creek police. I always went into an investigation with an open mind, not ready to judge until I had all the evidence to determine what happened.

There were a few things I wanted to look at again after we finished with the autopsies and I got the ME's thoughts. My stomach turned over thinking of him. Would we be able to navigate our job responsibilities with our previous entanglements staring us both in the face? We were professionals, so I was optimistic we would. But I couldn't get the image of his naked body out of my head.

The man's voice startled me from my thoughts.

"Well, I'm off today, so you'll have a different team with you," he said.

"As long as the scene's being held, I really don't need anybody there," I advised him while swirling some pancakes around in the buttery syrup while I eyed him. "What's your name?

"Chad, sorry, should have introduced myself. Do you think it's suspicious?" he asked.

I furrowed my brows. That was a very quick segue from name to weird question. "What would make you ask that?"

"I don't know." He shrugged.

I picked up my mug and looked at him over the rim. I don't remember him at all from yesterday. He was being nice enough, but a bit too nosy for my liking. He sat for the next few minutes after he said he was going to leave. I kept my conversation to a minimum and focused on my food.

"Well, I guess I better get back to it. Just coming off shift and wanted some breakfast before hitting the hay." He stood and dropped a couple of bucks on the table. "Was nice chatting with you."

"You too." I looked up at him and smiled.

He returned it and nodded. "I'm sure of it."

He left, and I ran over the conversation in my head. Getting to know people was difficult. And since I was somewhat of a closed book most times, it was challenging coming to a new place and trying to fit in.

After breakfast, I followed my GPS and pulled into the parking lot of the fire marshal's office. This would be my home base, along with whatever living arrangements I would secure. The building was kind of different. It had nice architecture and didn't really look like an office building.

It was surrounded by trees and strangely enough, it had vineyards behind it. I was unaware grapes grew in this area.

Oak Creek was a pretty place, at least what I've seen of it since I got here. Maybe it would work for me. I'd had another opportunity down in Florida Keys that was really pulling at me. I love it down there, so living and working in a beautiful place would be an absolute dream.

I climbed out of the truck, and the image of Taylor's face floated in my mind. Yes, Oak Creek did have some things going for it.

Chapter Four

Everything went fine at the fire marshal's office. They wanted me to work more remotely than in office, which was exactly what I preferred. Basically, I had a desk and a plug-in to Wi-Fi. All reports, files, photos, and everything I needed was on a secure network with firewalls. I was also provided with a tablet to use to interface with the office. I was impressed with the organization.

Now it was time for the postmortem on the three victims. On the drive to the PM, I had to bolster myself. It was not going to be pleasant. I'd be watchful on every little thing, taking photos to document as well. It was my responsibility to determine if it was arson after the coroner pronounced the cause of death and whether the victims were alive or deceased at the time of the fire.

My belly did a little tumble knowing I'd be standing across the table from Taylor, watching him work with the memory of our steamy weekend hanging between us.

It was a short drive, and I let out a sigh as I pulled into the fire marshal's parking spot. I smiled. It was nice to have my own space. I grabbed what I needed from the passenger seat and got out.

I paused and looked at the building. Taking a deep breath, let it out slowly.

"Here we go."

***

Once, inside, after passing through security and finding my way to the ME wing and the morgue, I was shown to a change room. Gowned up with protective clothing, cap, and face shield, I waited in the vestibule outside the autopsy suite.

My business attire wasn't the most attractive or alluring getup. That's why when I first started working in the field, I decided to indulge my passion for lingerie by wearing it under all this non-glamorous workwear.

I pulled the gloves on, now quite used to not poking a nail through the fingertips. I didn't keep my nails long or sharp, just a nice length and rounded. I held my hands in front of me; fingers splayed and inspected the purple gloves. All good.

Voices from down the hall reached me, and I turned to watch the team approach. They were also geared up like I was.

It was easy to find Taylor. He was the tallest and broadest of the bunch. I swallowed and fisted my hands. Memories would not leave me alone. This one was me with my arms wrapped around his shoulders, ankles locked behind his butt, my face buried into his neck as we fucked against the hotel room wall.

"Drea?" Taylor invaded my hot thoughts.

I blinked and stood taller, doing my best to force the image out of my brain.

"Ah, yes. How are you?" I looked at each member of the team and nodded, trying to settle myself down. I needed to get a grip and not have any more memories pop up.

"Alright then, let's get busy." Taylor pushed open the autopsy room doors and held them for us to pass. Three bodies lay draped on three separate tables. I drew in a deep breath seeing the two smaller ones.

"Is Shannon coming?" I asked as I positioned myself at the head of the three tables, waiting to see which one Taylor would start with.

"She should be here by now. We need her for the second victim." We all glanced over at the middle table.

I nodded and pulled my lips between my teeth. It didn't do for me to get emotional. Kids could do that to you.

"Right then, I'm going to start with the baby. He looked over to the members of his team. "Linda, Paul, you can begin with the mom." We all went to our respective tables. Once Shannon arrived, I expected we would then move to the middle child. Taylor reached down and gently pulled back the sheet covering the baby. I sucked in a breath and glanced up at him quickly when I heard him do the same.

"Doesn't matter how many times you do this, it does not get any easier." Taylor drew the sheet off and we stood looking down at the child.

He switched on the microphone and began his post-mortem. I watched, taking notes and photographs as he performed all the necessary steps.

The room was hushed except for the soft talking of Taylor and Linda. Both recorded their findings and verbalized them as the PMs progressed.

By the time Shannon arrived, we were halfway through,

and I was a little more controlled and able to remove myself from the emotional state that had almost taken over.

Shannon breezed into the room, and I knew it was her way to arrive with aplomb. I bit back a smile.

"Linda, you carry on while we meet with the forensic pathologist." Taylor was very professional. I was still surprised that he'd shifted from being a doctor to a pathologist. I wondered why?

"Right then, let's take a look." Shannon walked over to the middle table while Taylor and I stood on either side. Shannon looked at us both, drew in a breath, and said, "Let's get started."

She pulled back the sheet, and we all looked down at the body on the table that had once been a child. I drew in a breath. It was always tough with kids, and I dreaded those calls.

Shannon was completely focused, so when she spoke it startled me. "Did you find soot in the trachea of the other two victims?"

"Yes." Taylor replied in a low voice.

That meant they were alive during the fire.

"Any other impact trauma to the bodies?" Shannon was carefully opening the fisted hand of the child. In a hot fire the body goes into a pugilistic stance or posture, with hands curled into a fist and arms flexed to the body like a boxer.

"No gunshot or knife wounds."

Shannon nodded and she and Taylor discussed her findings as she worked. I stood back and continued to take notes even though I knew her report would be in-depth.

My gaze gravitated to Taylor. Why had he switched from being a doctor to a pathologist? He'd spoken at the conference in Denver. I remember being impressed with his talk on ER and trauma medicine. I remained silent and watched them work.

* * *

Finally, we were done and it had not been pleasant. We were all quiet as we went down the hall to the change room. Shannon was still in the autopsy suite, and the rest of us stripped off our protective gear and put everything in the biohazard bin.

I'd been impressed with Taylor's quiet expertise as he performed the autopsies. His movements were precise and respectful.

Shannon pushed open the door and joined us. She began chattering away, and I half listened, thinking about Taylor and the fire scene. My thoughts were less about the fire and more about recalling our sexcapades in Denver rather than where my thoughts should really be focused. Here. Now. The job. I couldn't help it though, and a slow burn spread along my veins.

"How long before you think you'll have results?" I asked Taylor

"Hopefully by the end of tomorrow. Toxicology will be a little bit longer." He ran his fingers through his short dark hair, and his icy-blue eyes caught mine. I couldn't look away. I was magnetized and forgot the question I was about to ask.

"Uh, right. I was glad to see we found most of the bones, but I would like to get back to the scene to look a little more."

I pulled my gaze from him to Shannon.

"Yes, I do too."

"I'm going back now. Did you want to join me?"

Shannon looked at the time. "Really? Now? The scene will be there tomorrow morning you know. They won't release it until they get the go-ahead, so tomorrow will still be good."

I thought about it. "Okay, you're right. But early, okay?"

"Okay, early. Where are you staying?" she asked as she pulled on her jacket.

"At the Courtyard." I threw a quick glance at Tyler, but he had his back turned to us.

"Okay, I'm the B&B. We could have dinner somewhere in between."

"You know what? If we're going to the scene early, I'd rather get back to my room and sleep. I'm bushed."

"Aw, party pooper. Fine, we'll go tomorrow then."

We agreed, and I closed up my kit, ready to go. I felt Taylor's presence and glanced at him.

"Drea." My name on Taylor's lips sent a delightful thrill down my spine. "How about we connect tomorrow? I can let you know when the reports are done."

"Yes, good idea." I took a card from my wallet and handed it to him. "Here, so you don't have any trouble reaching me."

Our gazes lingered.

"Thanks." He put the card in his wallet.

I was finally able to pull my eyes away and hitched my bag on my shoulder.

We all walked down the hall to the exit, and Taylor held the doors for us. I gave everyone a smile.

"Okay, talk to you later."

I stepped past Taylor and followed Shannon out to the parking lot, careful not to look back.

"Okay, is there something going on there I need to know about?" she asked me as she tossed her gear into the trunk of her car.

Wow, that was the million-dollar question, and I did not have an answer for her.

Chapter Five

Visiting the scene this morning hadn't revealed any further discoveries, and I was able to determine the cause as non-suspicious, electrical. Such a shame, and very tragic for the family. I was looking forward to meeting Shannon for dinner. Something that I hadn't done in ages. I was excited to go out even if it was a little unnerving being in a new place.

But stepping outside my comfort zone was what it was all about, like coming to Oak Creek. I'd been ready to move on from where I was. I never seem to stay long anywhere, and I was okay with that.

As I drove over to the pub, I thought about the cat. Cinder. That's what I'll call him if I end up keeping him. Keeping him would be a commitment though, which was something I usually shied away from.

I drove my truck into the pub's parking lot and was surprised that it was so full. I found a spot off to the side under a tree and made sure I locked my door.

Music spilled out into the parking lot. It was loud but had a beat that already seeped into my soul. I like dancing, especially to the blues. It really got the groove going in me, but it usually took a few drinks to get me on dance floor.

Why? I wasn't shy. At least, I didn't think I was. Dancing wasn't the same as karaoke. To be up there singing all by myself made me cringe. With all eyes on you, I just couldn't do it. Good on those that good, but me? There was no way anyone could get me up to sing.

The door slammed shut behind me, and I blinked to adjust my vision to the dim lighting. The place was packed, and I felt like every eye was on me.

I threw a glance around the room, looking for Shannon. A waving hand caught my eye, and I smiled. It was just like her to find a table in the middle of the room where she could be seen.

"Great spot you got here," I said as I slid into the seat across from her.

She laughed. "I knew you'd love it. Even if you don't know anybody in town, you can bet they know you. You might as well let yourself be seen."

"Great." I glanced around, and sure enough, a few people were looking at me. I smiled at those that were and was grateful the rest of the crowd were busy with their food and drinks.

"So are you going to tell me what brought you to Oak Creek or are you keeping it a deep, dark secret?" That was Shannon, getting to the heart of the matter right off the hop.

I shrugged. "Are you kidding me? Don't you remember telling me about the opening?"

Shannon sputtered over her beer and then laughed. "Oh, yeah. I did, didn't I? That was ages ago. I didn't think you were going to follow it up."

"Well, I did." I rolled my eyes, and she shrugged her shoulders, grinning.

I scanned the floor for a waitress and signaled her. I needed a drink something fierce. I wasn't ready for Shannon's interrogation, and liquid fortification might help.

"Dunno. It's just the way I grew up." I tried to inject a bit of humor into my tone, but I'm not sure it came out exactly the right way.

The waitress put my beer in front of me, and I grabbed it to take a long drink. Nice way to stop the conversation. Even though I was good friends with Shannon, it was a topic I preferred not to discuss. My growing up had been painful, surviving the fire that took our house and my dad, everything that followed wasn't something I like to rehash.

"Interesting though, that we were both at the same call." I decided to make a bit of small talk to redirect her.

"My area is quite wide, so being here wasn't as much of a fluke for me as it is for you," she said over the rim of her glass.

A plate of nachos she must have ordered before I arrived was put in front of us.

"Whoa, I didn't realize how hungry I was." I reached for a very cheesy chip loaded with meat and jalapeños. The spicier the better. I topped it with dollop of sour cream, popped it in my mouth, and closed my eyes savouring the flavour

"I don't how you can eat that hot stuff." Shannon picked off some peppers and threw them on my side of the platter. I picked one up and popped it in my mouth, laughing when Shannon curled up her nose at me.

We fell silent for the next little while as we ate. I looked around the restaurant to see if I recognized anybody from the fire. Through the crowd, I noticed one familiar face. It was the guy who came over to my table when I was at the diner for breakfast the other day. I don't think he'd seen me yet.

"So, do you think you could settle down here?" Shannon asked before taking a big scoop of sour cream on her loaded chip and putting it into her mouth.

"It's possible. I won't know until I've been here a while."

She shook her head and reached for another chip, quickly flicking the pepper onto my side of the platter.

"Interesting. I heard you also got asked to go down to Key West. How did that play out? What made you pick here when you wanted to be there?"

I took a napkin and wiped the sour cream I felt hanging on my lip and took a swig of beer, trying to decide how to answer that.

"Good question really. As much as I love the Keys, there was just something that drew me here. I wasn't supposed to be anywhere until next week, but they called and asked me to come and check the place out early."

"So you haven't signed a contract?" She sat back and ran her hands through her long, curly red hair, gathering it up into a bundle before letting it drop. She watched me with her pale-blue eyes, like a turquoise sea, and I knew that behind her beauty was a very sharp mind. She didn't miss a thing.

"Yes, I did, but you know me, it doesn't mean I'm tied here." She nodded, hopefully satisfied with my answer. Even though I still had no clue what I was going to do long term. That was me. Wandering aimlessly. I had to admit Oak Creek wasn't so bad. At least my first impression of it had been good.

And then there was Taylor. Him being here had been a totally unexpected surprise. It was good to see him and know he was here, and she was enjoying reliving the memories of their smoking-hot history, but that's all it was.

My mind drifted back to our time in Denver. The heat we made didn't hold a candle to the jalapeños on this plate of nachos. We'd agreed it was a one-time thing though. No ties. Just a weekend to enjoy each other and the pleasures of the body. We'd both been very happy with the way we left things and hadn't exchanged contact info.

Something snapped in my face, and I blinked, refocusing my thoughts.

Shannon was snapping her fingers. "Where are you, girl? You were miles away a minute ago. And by the look on your face, it was a pretty pleasant trip."

I waved my hand dismissively. It's best to keep the history between Taylor and I private.

"Do you think we're going to finish all these nachos?" I asked as I reached for another one and added a couple of peppers. I wasn't a fan of the salsa, it was overpowered with cilantro.

"If we don't, we can take it back to either your place or mine.

"Do you have a permanent home here?" I asked her.

She gave me a peculiar look. "That's the strangest question. Why would you differentiate between home and a permanent home?"

"Maybe because I've never had a permanent one." I laughed and then clammed up when the image of Taylor invaded my thoughts. I dug into my bag for a napkin when I saw the envelope someone left at the front desk.

"What's that?" Shannon tilted her head so she could see the handwriting on the front.

"You tell me." I handed her the envelope. She looked at it, holding it like it might contain anthrax or something.

"Have you looked inside?"

I shook my head. "It was left at the front desk, and I forgot it was in my bag until now."

She carefully opened the envelope and peered inside. "Drea, this is creepy. It says, *I'm watching you, and you'll never see me.*" She dropped the envelope with a little yelp. "What the hell! You have to call the police." She pushed the envelope back to me.

"Holy shit." I wasn't sure what to do. It freaked me out. "Nothing more has happened since I got it, and I forgot about it until now."

"I think you really need to tell the cops." She looked around the bar.

"What are you doing?"

"Looking for a cop," she said and then waved her arm.

"Oh, come on. Not here." I didn't want to discuss it with anyone other than Shannon right now.

A guy rose from a table and came over. "Hey, Shannon, fancy meeting you here." He had a nice smile.

"Trev, it's been a while. Sorry to intrude on your evening, but I'd like you to give your opinion to my friend here. This is Andrea. She's the new fire marshal."

"How are you?" He reached to shake my hand. "What can I help you with?"

"Nothing really." I shot Shannon a look and reached for the envelope, but she was quicker than me and snatched it.

"This. Someone left this at the front desk of her hotel."

Trev frowned. He looked at the front and then gingerly opened the envelope to look inside.

I groaned.

"See, he's cautious too." Shannon raised her eyebrows to drive the point home.

"Whatever," I said under my breath.

"Your room number?" he asked, pointing to the number on the front.

"Yes."

"Nothing else? No more notes or anything to alarm you?"

"No, nothing."

"I'm off duty now, but you should file a report just so it's on record."

"See! I told you." Shannon was proud of herself for being right.

"Really?" I wasn't impressed.

"Yes, better safe than sorry." Trev put it down on the table.

"But what can you do? Nothing, right?" I challenged him.

He took it well and smiled "No, not right now. But keep it and put it in another envelope to preserve any prints that may be on it. Try not to touch it anymore."

Trev gave me his card in case I wanted to talk further. I nodded, now feeling uneasy. It was difficult to finish the rest of our evening without thinking about the note.

* * *

I swiped my keycard on the lock. A dark room greeted me, and it was cold. The air con must have been turned down low.

I flipped the switch, and the darkness was chased away. I had a routine when in a hotel room and was religious about it. I locked the door and did a jam at the bottom, covered the peephole, checked the closet, the shower, behind the curtains and under the bed. It was a ritual. One that I started doing after being stalked by an arsonist.

In this line of work, there are crazies. One of my jobs is to determine how a fire started and if there was anyone involved.

I turned on the TV and found a channel that looped Buddha flute music. Another one of my rituals was setting out all my devices and plugging them in to charge. I always had a multi-port power/USB charger with me. I had too much stuff to just rely on hotel outlets.

I let out a sigh and turned, leaning my hip on the drawer unit.

It was a nice hotel, comfortable enough, and the bed looked cozy. All I wanted to do right now was shower and cocoon in the cozy duvet and pile of pillows.

Since arriving in Oak Creek, I'd been on the go nonstop. The dinner with Shannon had been a nice break and needed, but she'd asked some difficult questions. Then there was the police officer she'd dragged over to our table.

I'll think about it tomorrow.

Her questions, I had to admit, had forced me to take a hard look at my life. Changes I might want to make. I'd coasted along the last few years and honed my craft. Earned a reputation that had me called to scenes in a variety of places.

Again, I wondered if I should create my own company. I love what I do and grimaced a bit when I thought about my nomadic life. I never stayed anywhere long enough to put down roots.

I kicked off my shoes and stripped down to my underwear, my long nail caught on the lacy panties. I was careful to not poke a hole. I inspected the nail. There was a catch in it. I'd file it and would then have to find a good nail salon. It was just a little thing, going to a spa, and just for me. I still liked to have my girlie moments.

My thoughts slid back to Denver and Taylor. I'd been wearing some nice lingerie then and had been quite happy that I was. But it hadn't stayed on long enough for him to notice.

I almost moaned. Being with him had been the most erotic moment of my life. There was something about him that allowed me to drop all my walls and let him in. Something I hadn't done prior or since. I'd almost missed the session on blast investigative techniques, which was the main reason I was there.

Our encounter was definitely unplanned and delightfully naughty. I honestly didn't think I had it in me, but there was something freeing about being with Taylor.

I walked into the bathroom and turned on the shower, remembering the weekend. I'd been sad when it was time to say goodbye. Water rained on my face and hair, sluicing down my body. It wasn't difficult to pretend my hands were Taylor's as I soaped and rinsed myself.

This was getting dangerous. It was far too easy to conjure up erotic thoughts and let my mind run away with them. I stepped out of the shower, pulled a towel around me, and wound my hair up in a second towel.

The past had come back to haunt me. We'd made a deal back then that it was just that weekend, nothing more. No complications, no entanglements, just two lonely people enjoying each other, needing comfort and connection.

I pumped face lotion onto my fingertips and massaged it in. Staring into the mirror, I wondered if I'd changed much to him. He was even hotter now than he'd been then.

Our conversation had been minimal. The connection between us clicked so strongly at the time. Memories reared up...his hands...mouth, on me, in me, and mine on him. My hand trembled, and I knocked the toothbrush against my teeth. Damn, I was getting flustered, and that simply wouldn't do.

What were the odds that we'd both wind up in the same town years later? Oh, about a million to one.

I dropped the towels and crawled between the sheets naked.

"This feels wonderful," I murmured into the pillows and snuggled deeper into the cushiony bed.

But my mind was wide awake. I flicked off the light and closed my eyes, seeing Taylor's face etched into my eyelids.

Maybe my stay in Oak Creek was going to be much shorter than I anticipated.

* * *

Taylor put a few beers in the tin bucket full of ice, popped one open, and tossed the cap on the counter before he went out to the front porch. Nothing like a cold beer on a hot day. He sat down on the chair and propped his bare feet on an antique wooden box. He'd found it in the garage, along with a treasure trove any antique hunter would relish. For him, it was just a footrest.

He tilted his head, and while he took a long drink from the bottle, he made a mental note that the porch ceiling needed repainting.

"Ahhh, that hit the spot," he told no one in particular. His words carried away on the breeze.

What a day. He'd recognized his unsettled feelings and had to ground himself. It wasn't like him to feel edgy while doing a PM. Once he'd left working in the ER and trauma, he'd managed to keep those feelings under control. With the help of therapy.

Did he miss the frenzy of ER and surgery? Maybe

sometimes. The adrenaline rush, the split-second decisions required with a trauma, the patients sliding in and out of his life had all become a blur.

Except one.

He adjusted himself on the chair and cleared his throat. The familiar tightening around his heart had got much better over the last year, but it was never far behind when thoughts of his sister-in-law and niece burst into his mind.

He glanced around. No one was paying him any attention. He was just another guy sitting on another porch with a beer. He was good. No one was around.

This was the part he hated most. The hypervigilance. Always on high alert to his surroundings. Double-checking the locks on the doors, going over his reports to make sure he hadn't made a mistake. He was meticulous and never found any errors.

But it was the nightmares. They played over and over in his brain.

That's why he didn't sleep.

For the millionth time, he thought of all the if-onlys. He knew it was the PM he'd done on the victims of the fatal fire that had triggered him. The mom and her kids.

It was always the kids.

His gaze followed the fluttering of a few birds that hid in the branches of the huge tree on his front lawn. They chattered away, jumping from branch to branch, living their own lives. Maybe he should get a bird feeder. He liked seeing nature in his garden.

Taylor was content sitting here. He'd been invited out to the bar after work. Back in the day, he'd be there with bells on, but not so much anymore. He did his best to avoid social gatherings now.

A car drove down the street and pulled into the

driveway across the road. A family spilled out of the family van, husband, wife, and three kids. Their laughter reached him, and Taylor smiled. The man looked at him and raised a hand after wrangling the kids. Taylor returned the gesture.

The kids ran into the house, but not before their dog escaped and zoomed around the front lawn full of happiness. The kids called the dog, who bolted back in the house in a flurry of barks and excited screams from the children. The front door shut, and the sounds of family life silenced.

Taylor pressed his lips together and drew in a deep breath. Sounds he doubted he'd ever have in his life. He lifted his beer and stared at the label.

"Ah, fuck it." He guzzled the rest, fished out another icy bottle and popped it open.

Taylor stretched out on the chair, resting his head.

He liked this street. It was more family oriented than what he'd expected though, with kids on their bikes playing on the street. There was always laughter and shouts. He liked that the street was busy. Maybe the kids were a bit too young for devices and social media. Either way, it was great to see them outside.

He lifted the bottle and took a swig, gazing at the neat, older homes. Most had been nicely renovated, as far as he could tell from the outside. The street was shady, with large lots and privacy. A perfect retreat at the end of the day. He'd snapped this place up when his agent showed him the listing. Buying it sight unseen hadn't bothered him.

The change from ER doc to medical examiner hadn't bothered him either, but it did necessitate a move. A move that Taylor refused to admit was running. Running from his failure. If he put it behind him, he could start fresh. At least that's what he continued to tell himself.

About six months after Denver, there'd been an incident that had changed his life. Well everyone's life for that matter. The world had shut down because of the pandemic. He'd watched so many people die, colleagues, friends, family and strangers. But when it touched his family and he could do nothing about it except watch his sister-in-law struggle and ultimately lose her battle in his care. He blamed himself.

How could anyone overcome that? Her loss was devastating for him professionally and personally. He'd accepted it, through therapy, that he wasn't to blame. But the underlying guilt never seemed to go away.

Taylor had lost his light. Confidence. He'd begun to hesitate when victims arrived in the ER. Unable to treat them, he'd stepped back, taken a leave, and made decisions.

He loved medicine, but he just couldn't do the ER anymore. It had taken one death too many, and the pandemic had made it all just too much. Once things returned to the new normal, he had to make a change.

The dead couldn't die, but he could still help them. Help the family find a sense of closure. So he became a medical examiner.

Finding the whys of the death fit with him much better than finding the ways to prevent death. In order to keep himself in the medical field, this was where he needed to be.

He hadn't made the switch lightly. It wasn't like Taylor to make a hasty decision. He'd thought about it from every angle until he was satisfied with his decision.

A bunch of boys on bikes raced past his house on the road, their shouts and laughter proof of a good time. He was grateful to see they all wore helmets.

Taylor sighed and rested back on the porch chair. Yep, this would do.

His thoughts drifted to Drea. It was an understatement

to say he'd been shocked when he saw her at the scene. Her zest for life and passion had left a very distinct mark on his soul. Their time together in Denver had been the most amazing few days of his life. He thought about her every so often after their fling.

What was she doing right now? Likely not sitting on the porch like he was, probably out having a good time. Was she out partying? Possibly at Beatniks.

He wondered if she still was as wild and passionate as when he knew her. She'd been very professional when he'd seen her at the fire scene and at the postmortem today.

Was she in a relationship now? Married? Have kids? Taylor was surprised at the mild pang of jealousy, which made no sense at all. How could he be jealous over someone he'd only spent a few days with years ago. Yet here he was thinking about it.

They would continue to cross paths, both for this fire and future ones, and he didn't want there to be awkward tension between them.

One thing he did know, he wouldn't be able to look at her and not remember their weekend together. He finished the last of his beer and tried to recall the subject matter of the conference. His was medical, but hers...

Then he remembered.

She was on an explosion and blast course. He'd been quite impressed.

Taylor chuckled. Their weekend had definitely been explosive.

Chapter Six

The next morning, desperate for a coffee, I was looking forward to heading out to a recommended coffee shop. Apparently, the pastries were to die for and the coffee was like being transported to Hawaii. I was just about salivating for a cup.

Honu was the name. Apparently, it meant turtle in Hawaiian, and the beans came from Hawaii. I hurried across the parking lot, feeling much like a pack mule with all my bags slung around my shoulders.

I had so much on my mind that all my thoughts were in chaos. If I was planning on staying here, I had to find somewhere better to stay than the hotel. Even though my costs are covered, I simply couldn't have more than a few nights here. I have to find somewhere else less hotel-y. Maybe the B&B Shannon was staying at? I'd ask around for some suggestions, but so far nothing had turned up.

Reports on the fire were still coming in, and I had a load of paperwork to do. But, I needed to fit in a drive to Wags & Whiskers, which wasn't far from the hotel. I was eager to see the little guy and give the kitty a snuggle. I'd stop by tomorrow.

The day was already warm and I puffed out a breath, then stopped dead in my tracks.

"What the..." I couldn't believe what I was seeing.

I pulled the straps of my bags over my head and dropped them by the passenger door. My plans for the morning had taken a sudden turn.

Coffee.

Go to the office.

Check for reports.

But now I had this to deal with.

Last night, after my dinner with Shannon, I'd parked the truck under the light closer to the main entrance, figuring it would be safer there.

Apparently not.

I crouched down to look at the tire. It was fine yesterday and today it's flat. I pressed the tire with my fingers and found a big slice. Someone had slashed it. Who on earth would do such a thing? And why?

There was some etching on the side of the truck as well. A chill ran down my spine. Had this been random, or targeted?

I swore under my breath, stood, and glanced around the lot to see if any other vehicles were vandalized, or if anyone sketchy was lurking close by. I'd learned that offenders liked to hide and watch the reaction of their victims. I wasn't going to show my defeat. No way would I give them that satisfaction if they were still watching.

I knew the damage had to be reported. The keying wasn't really bad, but still...and the tire!

I unlocked the truck, put my gear inside, and went

around to the back to pull out the spare tire. I really couldn't believe this was happening right now.

The spare was a full-size, no donut for this vehicle. And it was heavy. I'd taught myself to change a tire years ago, because you never know when you might have to. And I wasn't about to be a helpless female.

Only I hadn't done it on a big 4x4 dually. It might prove to be a little more challenging. I leaned the tire against the fender and placed the jack beside it. As I expected, it wasn't easy. I decided to call roadside assistance and was advised they'd be here in about twenty-five minutes.

I put my phone back on the seat, absolutely craving that coffee I'd promised myself. I ran my fingers over the etching in the paint and leaned back down to see if there were any words.

"Having a bit of trouble there?" a male voice said, and a man came around from the back of the truck.

I stood up quickly, and the blood rushed from my head. I steadied myself with a hand against the truck, blinked, and looked at him. "A bit. But I'm good."

"That really sucks. You want me to give you a hand?" the guy asked. He had on a baseball cap, sunglasses, and a big beard.

I looked at him and wasn't sure what to say. On one hand, I was ready to yell hell yes, please do this for me, but on the other hand, I was hesitant. For one thing, I didn't like to show any weakness, and for another, the guy kind of creeped me out. I didn't know him, and he could be just a nice bystander. I made a quick decision.

"Thanks for the offer, but I've called roadside assistance. They'll be here shortly." He stepped forward, and I retreated. My instincts went on high alert.

"If you're sure." His voice was gravelly, and he didn't look familiar at all.

"Absolutely, thanks for offering." I saw a tow truck pull into the lot and relief washed through me. "Ah, here we go. They've arrived."

The guy gave me a smile. "Anytime." He turned and sauntered around the rear of the truck with a quick glance back at me.

I had the urge to run back and make sure nothing had been taken, and to see which way he went, or if he got into a vehicle, but the tow truck driver was getting out of his vehicle.

"Hi, aren't you a sight for sore eyes," I told the driver. He was probably in his late thirties and rather attractive. This town grew them hot.

He laughed. "It's nice to be needed. Nice truck. Let's get you all fixed up so you can be on your way."

The man took a quick glance at the situation and immediately went to work. He was finished in no time. I'd probably have been here for hours. It certainly was worth having roadside assistance, even if the company paid for it.

"You're all set." He stood and grabbed a rag from his truck to wipe his hands. "Somebody got at it, I see."

"It looks like it. I have no clue why." I handed him my roadside assistance card, and he wrote down the numbers.

"People can be weird." He tipped his pen in the direction of the logo on the truck. "As I'm sure you know." He gave me my card back.

"Only too well." I closed my wallet and put it in my bag on the passenger seat. "Thank you, you're a lifesaver."

He smiled. "That's what I'm here for. Maybe I'll see you around Oak Creek."

"Maybe you will." I grinned and watched him drive off. He waved as he turned out of the hotel lot.

He'd put the ruined tire in the back of the truck, and I went around to close things up. Nothing looked out of the ordinary. The eight-foot commercial cap had side-locking cabinets—without the key you weren't getting in—the back had a slide-out bed tray to access the tools inside.

It was a big mother, and parking in a city can be challenging. I hadn't found a drive-through big enough for it. Speaking of drive throughs, I needed that coffee.

* * *

I found the coffee shop and pulled into the parking lot. There was a drive-through, but I'd have to check it out to see if the truck would fit.

I maneuvered the big 4x4 to a spot large enough. I climbed down and reached in for my wallet. A purse really wasn't my style, and I didn't carry one when I worked. It wasn't the best look with my work uniform, which consisted of tactical pants, black belt, green patch safety shoes and logoed shirt.

Cool air rushed at me once inside, and I felt like I'd been transported to the South Pacific. It was glorious. Mock palm trees, tables, and decor with Hawaiian touches made me want to sit here all morning, or better yet, drop everything and fly to Hawaii.

There was a waterfall mural on the far wall, soft Hawaiian music and lapping waves came from the hidden speakers. It was calming, and I swear I could almost smell coconuts and flower leis. My morning drama drifted away like a lei floating on the waves. I decided I loved the place without even having tasted the coffee or food.

It was obviously a favorite of the locals. The place was packed, and I found my way into the line that snaked along another wall lined with nostalgia from the islands including photos of old-world Hawaii. It made waiting to place your order go swiftly.

A waist-high wall with tropical plants separated the line from the tables. A nice touch.

I smiled at the others in the line. My truck and the uniform sometimes raised conversation as neither were very subtle. Especially with the recent fatal fire that had been in the news. I didn't recognize anyone, but then my world hadn't really expanded yet to the greater Oak Creek.

I shifted focus to the menu and decided on a macadamia, coconut confection. They asked if I wanted it hot or iced. I pondered... Oh, decisions. Ultimately, I decided on hot. Amazing-looking pastries with Hawaiian names waited behind the glass and wood display. My taste buds sprang to life, and I couldn't decide which to get.

"Would you like anything else with that?" the barista asked me.

"Most definitely, my sweet tooth calls. But I can't decide. How about you pick a few and surprise me?"

She lit up. "I love it when guests ask me to do that."

I was glad I'd made her happy. We needed happy in the world.

"Are you a firefighter?" she asked when she handed me my bag of treats.

"No, fire investigator." I handed her money to pay for my order.

"Oh! I've never known a woman... I'm sorry, I didn't mean—

"It's okay. There's not many of us."

"It must be very interesting."

I nodded. "Yes, it is."

She leaned forward, and in a conspiratorial whisper asked, "Did you go to the fire where the family, er, well..." She trailed off, probably unsure what to say.

"I was there. Very tragic." I didn't want to talk about it and moved down the line to wait for my drink.

I heard voices at the door and turned. My heart leapt into my throat when I saw Taylor. The reaction caught me completely by surprise. I couldn't look away from him while he chatted with another guy. He was an attractive man and he'd only gotten more handsome since we were together in Denver. I hadn't really noticed it at the fire, or at the autopsy, but now, I most certainly did. His dark short-cropped hair made his piercing blue eyes pop. The jeans and shirt he wore emphasized his fit body, but all I could see was him in his naked glory.

I cleared my throat and closed my eyes for a moment, an aching, sweet heat spread through me, and I found it difficult to draw in a breath.

Serious proof that I'd been celibate for way too long. Especially when reminded of...

I shook my head. *Get a grip, girl. I'd have to, because we'd be bumping into each other in a small town like Oak Creek.*

Was I ready to talk with him? Or should I just take my order and run? My name was called.

I made my way between the other guests and took my order. "Thank you."

"You're welcome. We hope to see you back soon."

I nodded. "You can count on it." I turned to make my way through people waiting and nearly bumped right into Taylor. I froze and stared up at him.

He smiled, and I found myself grinning back at him.

"You found our secret place," he said, keeping me caught in his gaze.

My heart battered in my chest, and I was puzzled for a moment. Our place? "Oh, you mean the town's secret place," I answered him.

"Yes, this place has been a hit since it opened a few months ago. You can count on everything being authentic and delicious." He shuffled forward in the line, and I turned in my place so we could continue talking.

"It certainly is unique. A nice change from normal coffee shops."

He nodded. "Are you in a rush to go anywhere? If you're not, maybe we can sit and enjoy our Hawaiian delicacies at a table."

The intensity of his gaze nearly melted me inside. "Ah, yeah, I think I could find some time."

"Did you want to grab that table by the window while I get my order?"

I was captivated by his grin and felt like a schoolgirl. All the memories of Denver rushed back again, and I knew that us being together in the same room could have dangerous side effects. "Sure, no problem," I basically muttered it, still feeling rather flustered.

Heat flushed my face, and I turned partly so he couldn't see my blush as I made my way to the table before someone else got it.

I sat, rested my chin on my hand and watched him, keeping my head down slightly so it didn't look like I was staring at him. Why was I being such a freak? It wasn't like we didn't know each other, even if we had met years ago and only spent time doing things of a sexual nature. I couldn't throw off the longing raging through me.

A few minutes later, he walked over to the table, and I

enjoyed every moment of it. He moved easily, with a rolling gait that emphasized his size, strength, and maleness. I flushed again, this time with muscle memory of the desire I'd felt when we were together. He'd lifted me, grabbed my ass, and pressed me into the wall. A soft breath escaped me, and I quickly grabbed my coffee to take a sip. Oh God, I hope he didn't hear my almost moan.

He sat and looked quietly at me. My feelings reflected in his gaze. How would we get through this? Working in close proximity would be almost unbearable. Unless I was able to firmly control myself. We had to keep things purely professional.

"So here we are," he murmured in a low voice and then took a drink from his cup.

"Uhm, yup...here we are."

I could have died from sounding so dull.

Drea sitting across the table in the middle of a coffee shop seemed very surreal to him. This woman had dropped back into his life and thrown him right off-kilter. He thought she couldn't appear sexier than when they were in Denver, but she was just as hot in her work clothes.

But maybe that was why he found her attractiveness even more powerful today, now that they'd spent time together and shared the kind of passion they shared. To see her now years later was very compelling.

He'd thought about her a lot since the fire, almost to the point of distraction. Through the grapevine, he'd heard about the note she'd received. He wanted to ask her about it but chose to wait and see if she'd say anything.

"So are we going to talk about the elephant in the room?"

Drea said and lifted the coffee to her lips, peering at him over the rim of her cup.

He knew exactly what she was referring to. "Sure." He returned her smile and waited for her to make the first move.

"We can't let this be awkward." She held the cup closer to her mouth.

He followed the rim of the cup to where her lips reached the edge, and he hardened, remembering the sweet torment her lips had put him through.

"No, it definitely can't be awkward."

"Nor can we ignore that it happened." Her voice lilted up in somewhat of a question.

"No, I couldn't ignore that. It was a very special weekend for me," he admitted, and it was as if admitting his feelings, meant being vulnerable and vulnerability only led to emotional pain.

Her eyebrows rose, and he wondered what was racing around inside her brain.

"It was for me too, and not something I expected to happen. Nor did I ever expect to see you again."

He shook his head. "Me either. How we handled it at the time, our conference fling, was satisfactory to both of us, wasn't it?"

"Yes, it was. More than satisfactory, in fact"

They sat in silence for a few minutes, and he wondered what she was thinking.

"These are really good." She held up one of the pastries from the bag and held it out to him. ""

"Thank you." He reached in and took out one of the tarts.

"They taste like vacation." She closed her eyes in exaggeration.

He laughed, enjoying their banter and her humor. "They certainly do. Have you been to Hawaii?"

"No, it's always been on my list. But after being here, I think it's just been bumped to the top."

He had to stop himself from saying that maybe they could go there together for another weekend. He couldn't believe it crossed his mind. Way too soon for that!

She finished her tart and licked her fingers glancing at her watch.

"Oh, I have to go." She gathered up her things and stood. He did as well.

"I'm glad I bumped into you. I suppose I'll see you when the report is finalized." He told her as he walked out the door. He nodded to some people he knew sitting in a booth near the exit.

"Yes, for sure. Let me know when it's ready and I can come by to get a copy."

"Sure. Not yet though, but I have your info if you want them emailed."

"Okay, thanks." He walked her to her truck and ran his finger along the scratch.

"And that was how my day started. Flat tire and keyed truck."

"Nope, definitely not a way to start the day."

"Agreed, the tire was slashed, and this was obviously deliberate."

He looked at her surprised and concerned. "Really? You think so?"

She nodded. "It's possible. And it wouldn't be the first time."

"I didn't realize that your line of work is that dangerous."

He held the door open for her, and she climbed in. "Oh, it can be. If it's arson, I have to go to court and present my findings. Some people don't like it, but I figure people who start fires need to be caught and put away."

He pointed to the scratch. "Maybe report it to the police?"

She gave him a sharp look. "Of course, I need to get an occurrence number for the insurance."

"Good, I feel better for you already. Take care and watch your back."

She smiled at him, and Taylor liked how it made him feel. It was a good feeling. He wanted to see her again, only next time for longer.

"Don't worry, I always do."

Chapter Seven

While driving over to Wags & Whiskers, using my GPS, I replayed the conversation Taylor and I had over our morning coffee. So far, we hadn't really touched on Denver. I wondered if we did, if it would set off some kind of explosive episode.

Because Denver had definitely been fiery. I blew out air from my pursed lips. Yeah, we'd have to talk about it eventually. Part of me was excited, and the other part was a little scared.

Not frightened, but... What...? Scared we wouldn't be able to keep our hands off each other? Scared he'd reject me? Scared he had a family?

"Just stop," I told myself and glanced at the navigation screen to double-check I made the right left turn. I had other things to worry about.

Like the cat.

I finally was able to check up on him and looked forward to seeing the little guy. I always had a bag of dog food in the truck, because I come across dogs at scenes often. The food helped to coax them out, and in other cases, I'd feed those that needed it. I didn't like to see the strays at scenes. I wished I could bring them all home with me and it hurt my heart that I couldn't.

I pulled onto the street and drove slowly, reading the street numbers. It wasn't hard to find Wags & Whiskers. The sign outside was easy to spot. I parked the truck on the street in front of the house and walked up to the business. The sign said come on in, and so that's what I did.

Mel called from the wash station. "I'm back here. Come on through."

I did and smiled when I saw she was bathing a huge sheep dog. It looked like both of them were getting a bath.

"Yeah, this guy's a bruiser. But I love him," Mel said. "He comes in fairly regularly to keep himself looking so handsome. You must be Drea?" She rolled right from one subject to the next, and I felt energy just pouring off her.

"Yep, that's me. Thanks so much for taking care of the cat. And I'm sorry I couldn't get by sooner." I wandered over a little closer to the station but was careful since I didn't want to get wet from the spray. I didn't have a change of clothes and need to do laundry.

"Pssft, don't worry about that. He's fine, little scared, and he was dirty, but I bathed him—"

"You bathed him? Isn't that kind of a dangerous escapade to do?"

"Don't worry. I suited up." Mel laughed. It was infectious, and I found myself laughing along with her. "Oh yeah, some cats are teddy bears for bathing, and others are hellcats. This guy was a hellcat. I have suitable attire to protect myself from teeth and claws."

"I'm sorry if he gave you a hard time, but thank you."

She nodded her head in the direction of a doorway. "Go through. He really is a sweetie."

I nodded and took a step to the door she indicated. It was a lovely room that overlooked a very nice backyard. I glanced around and found the black cat curled up on the back of the chair in front of the window. I walked over to him, and he opened his eyes. Not very wide, just enough to see I was approaching. He yawned, and his ears vibrated back with the force of the yawn. His front paws stretched out, exposing some very serious nails.

"So how are you, little guy?" Tentatively, I reached out and petted him, which he seemed to like. He pushed his head into my hand, so I felt more confident picking him up.

When I did, he put his paws on my chest and looked up at my face. He studied me, and I swear to God, the cat knew who I was. He let out a small meow and rubbed his head against my chin. I don't know if I was just being overly emotional, but I couldn't believe it when tears popped into my eyes.

I snuggled him tightly under my chin, and the fresh smell of his fur was so much better than the smoky stink from the other day when he'd cuddled into me.

"Oh, little guy," I whispered. "I'm so sorry that you were stuck in the house. But I am glad I found you. Do you want to come home with me?"

He began to purr. It was loud, and I rested my ear on his back as he crept up to my shoulder. Oh yeah, this guy is definitely coming with me. "I think I'll call you Cinder."

I turned and walked into the spa.

"Look at that," Mel said. "He's been very standoffish and aloof with everyone else. I bet he remembers you from when you saved him."

I glanced at her, and she gave me a soft smile, her head tilting to the side. "I think so too."

"You're keeping him, aren't you? Looks like his claws have hooked your heart." She must've noticed the expression on my face and the telltale signs of tears I'd just wiped away.

"Oh yeah, I think so. But I'm in a hotel right now, and I can't keep him there. I don't know what to do."

"He's welcome to stay here as long as you need, and you can come by anytime and see him. I have no problem with that whatsoever."

"That's very kind. Thank you."

It was the only logical choice at the moment. A niggle of worry took root in my belly though. That meant I'd have to find somewhere more permanent to live. I looked down at his sweet face. His eyes were closed, his nose was wet, and the purring coming from him was loud and contented. Yeah, I think he has taken my heart.

"I will bring some food around for him."

Mel shook her head. "You don't need to. I've got plenty."

"I insist. You've been so wonderful keeping him, and I want to contribute to his care until I'm able to bring him home. Oh, and I decided his name a moment ago. Cinder."

Mel laughed. "It's perfect. That's fine about the food. Whatever you like. Hey, I'm going to be having a barbecue, still figuring out the date, but I'd love for you to come. It will help you meet some people from around here. I throw barbecues every now and then, and it's time for another." She hosed off the sheepdog and covered him with a towel as he was about to give a great big shake. "Stand back, or you'll get a shower."

I backed up, and sure enough he shook. It was almost

like a slow-motion movie. The towel came off, and great arcs of hair and water spewed around him, reflecting in the light.

My phone pinged. I shifted Cinder to my other arm and reached in my pocket for it. I looked at the message.

"I'm sorry, but I have to leave. Should I just put him back in the room?"

"Sure, he seems to have claimed the back of the chair. He loves looking out the window and chirping to the birds at the feeder. He's welcome here as long as you need. I have more than enough space for him." She paused. "Fire call?"

"Yes. I must be going. Again, thank you."

"Anytime. Be careful," Mel called after me.

* * *

I was excited. I'd been a bit anxious on my first call when I arrived in Oak Creek. Now, for the second one, I felt more in my groove. I put the address into my GPS and followed the instructions.

It was about an hour away, so that kind of put a kibosh on my plans to organize my office and finish up the report on the first fire. I'd have to do that later, maybe finish it in my hotel room with some takeout.

My truck was always ready for a job. I kept it well stocked with everything needed. I usually kept a go-bag in case I needed a change of clothes, or an unexpected overnight stay. It figures I had to make a laundromat visit, so I was limited on essentials this time. I never knew when a call would come and when I'd have to go or where or if there would be delays. I wouldn't know until I arrived on scene, but initial reports were this had a lot of damage and was suspicious in nature.

Honu coffee shop was along the way, and I was

suddenly salivating for a pastry and big cup of jet fuel. As I rounded through the parking lot ready to give the drive-through a try, I was relieved to see it was wide enough and had no signage overhead so the truck fit. First time for everything!

I found myself searching the parking lot and looking through the windows for Taylor as I pulled into the lane.

I didn't think he wouldn't be there, but it didn't stop me from looking. Plus, seeing if he was around somehow made me feel a growing connection to Oak Creek. I knew someone, and it was a comfort, even if it was awkward.

The drive-through was quick, and I was soon rolling in the direction of the fire scene. I hadn't had confirmation if it was a fatal scene, but since it appeared suspicious, I'd been called.

If it was a fatal fire, Taylor and I would be crossing paths sooner than expected. A thrill of anticipation rippled through me. A clear indication that I did want to see him again.

Fifty-five minutes later, I pulled up to the building. It was still smoking and had hot spots.

I parked in front of the home. Firefighters usually made room for me so that my equipment was close to the scene. I was also thankful, because then it would be harder for anyone to try and steal items out of my truck.

I got out, and the captain came to greet me. She kept one eye on her fire crew while she talked.

"I guess the scene is yours now," she stated matter-of-factly, which wasn't really a question.

"I guess it is. Is there anything I need to know?" I asked.

She had her hand resting on the mic attached to the left side of her chest. She stood with a wide stance and stared at the house.

"It's abandoned and was scheduled for a demo years ago, just never been done. Sometimes the homeless get inside and there's drugs and squatting. We're not sure what set it off, but there are areas that look like MacGyver'd fire pits or stoves."

I nodded and followed her gaze. I wasn't really surprised to hear this.

"So far, no bodies have been discovered. My guess is when the fire started, they fled the building."

"Got it. I'm Andrea Trask. Drea."

She faced me and stuck out her hand "Nancy Crane. Nice to see a woman on the job." She smiled.

"Thanks. Glad to be here. Is the fire out?"

"It is. There are a few hot spots, and the structure is a bit iffy, so you'll have to be careful."

"Okay, thanks."

Her mic keyed up, and I turned away to finish getting my gear on while she answered.

"Drea, before you go in, it looks like there's asbestos in the building, so you'll have to be gowned and taped up. One of the crew will get you all set and have to come in with you. Hazmat is on the way as well."

"Right." Damn, being completely sealed up on a warm day would make this investigation a nightmare.

At the pumper, I waited while my wrists and ankles were taped so no asbestos could filter in. I had a mask on, and the hood was taped to it.

The firefighter double-checked everything, and I was ready to go. I didn't wear SCBA—self-contained breathing apparatus—because I'm not trained on it. After getting the layout of the building, I went inside. I swung my flashlight back and forth and switched on my helmet light. Hands-free is good, and I stowed the torch on my belt.

The place looked abandoned. No doubt about it. I worked my way through the rooms on the main floor. Nothing jumped out at me. However, I remained open-minded. There was a second level, and the fire crew said to stick to the wall going up and down the stairs, even though the fire had not progressed as far as the stairs. I climbed them with care.

Upstairs were more flop rooms with mattresses on the floor, garbage strewn about, and the makings of very unsafe cooking and heating tools.

Random cigarette butts littered the floor and could have easily started a fire. At the end of the hall, I opened a door that likely led to the attic.

This side of the building wasn't as damaged as the other side, but it was still charred and had water damage and smoke stains. It was obvious the fire had some impact here, but luckily enough, it was put out before it went up like a tinderbox.

I still had to go up to the attic. It was also littered with stained mattresses, moth-eaten sleeping bags, garbage, takeout boxes, drug paraphernalia, and booze bottles. The ceiling was coming down, likely from when the roof was ventilated, and insulation hung in wet hanks through the opening and in a pile on one of the mattresses.

Time to back out of here. I pointed to the ceiling, and the firefighter accompanying me nodded.

I'd finish my cursory first run through and it was time to head down into the basement.

Back on the main floor, it was clear the one side of the house was where the fire started. I looked for the entrance to the basement. The door was off its hinges and smoke still billowed up the stairs.

I followed the firefighter down the rickety steps. It was

even warmer down here, and I was sweating. My Tyvek suit stuck to my skin. I checked the taping on my wrists to see if the sweat had loosened the seal. I was good for a bit longer.

I didn't want to admit to myself I was overheating. I couldn't give in to it because then I risked being labeled as unfit. Unworthy of the job.

I'd earned respect from the fire fighters at my previous job, but I was new here and felt an overpowering urge to prove myself. I drew in a deep breath, put a steadying hand on the wall, and followed the firefighter into the dark, smoking basement.

The back of the room had a lot of thermal damage, and the fire had gone into the walls, finding its way up through the back of the house and fanning out from there. The old furnace was also in this area of the basement.

I nodded. Now I knew what I was looking for and needed photos, to make notes, take measurements, and I was dying of heat.

This was where the fire started, I was sure of it. There could have been an accelerant introduced to the furnace and set alight.

I pulled my camera from around my back, checked the setting for the level of darkness, and started taking photos. These images would help later when I dove into the findings.

While capturing images, I also scanned the floor, looking for anything that could've played a part in the start of the fire. There was so much debris around the furnace, I'd have to double-check for rags or anything else that could ignite.

I saw a lump of something on the far side of the basement. A-ha. And there it was. I took photos from all angles and tipped it over to see the bottom.

Red, intact, and unmelted. A gasoline jerrican.

Suddenly, I felt faint and swayed, lightheaded and hot.

The firefight took my arm. "Alright?" he asked.

I nodded and gently extracted myself from his grip. This was what I didn't want to happen.

Holding the jerrican, I couldn't see it any longer with the sweat pouring down my forehead and into my eyes. It stung, and I was unable to wipe it away without taking off my sealed-up gloves.

I carried on and continued along the back wall until we reached a vertical cinder block wall that looked much newer than the floor and original walls.

I looked up at the ceiling. The floor above was damaged and had come down in this area and pulled some of the insulation and drywall with it. I pushed it aside, and there was another door with what looked like an earthen floor behind the block wall.

The firefighter was beside me, and I pointed.

"Can we pull aside this debris to see what's behind it?"

He raised his halligan, and I stood back when he used it to pull away the pile.

"There's a door here," he said.

"Can you open it? We have to see inside."

He used the tool to pry open the door. Tentatively, I leaned over to look into the dark room. I needed the flashlight and took it from my belt to shine inside.

What the heck were we getting ourselves into?

I swung the flashlight back and forth, cautiously stepping over the mess.

I had a very bad feeling, but I ignored it and went farther into the room. I was really starting to heat up and feel nauseous inside the Tyvek suit. The firefighter was behind me. My eyes finally adjusted to the gloom. There was something in the rubble next to the wall.

I crouched to gently move around the ruins on the floor. It looked like burned drywall. I took a photo of it, because bone can also look like drywall.

As I leaned forward for a closer look, something hit me on the back. I let out a shout and rolled toward the door. Another section of the ceiling collapsed, bringing down pipes wrapped in old plumbing insulation. The building was the right age for asbestos insulation, and I was lucky I hadn't gone farther into the room. The object that caught my attention was now buried underneath all the rubble, insulation, and all kinds of debris from above. Just as I would've been if I'd been farther forward.

I pushed myself out of the pile and looked around for the firefighter. He was also extracting himself. He radioed for assistance and reached for my hand to help me out of the room.

Shortly, the basement was full of his fire crew, and they hustled us out.

I was panting, overly hot and feeling faint. I was either going to throw up in my mask or pass out if I didn't get out of this gear now.

"Okay, we gotta hose you. This is asbestos, and you need to be decontaminated." The lieutenant reached out his hand to grab mine.

"Asbestos." I was warned they thought there was asbestos, but now that it was confirmed, I simply had to get out of this gear.

My leg was a little sore as I followed the lieutenant out, and he was on his radio explaining the situation. Once up the stairs and outside, we'd be hosed off.

When we emerged into the daylight, I could see I was covered in dust. So was the firefighter behind me.

"Drea, you have to get hosed off. We want you to stand over here by your truck."

I stumbled off the porch. The heat, sweat, and concern for the asbestos almost had me in a panic.

"Hose me off!" I shouted at them.

"Yes, we will. Hazmat is on its way to decontaminate you. But we'll hose you down. Stand here and brace yourself. Arms up, eyes and mouth closed even with your mask on."

Nancy was giving me instructions, but I had to get out of the suit now, otherwise I'd be a goner. My vision was darkening around the edges, and I was about to pass out.

I ripped at the tape, frantically pulling at it. They shouted at me to stop, but I was frenzied to get out of the gear.

I freed my arms and pushed the suit down my body, flung off my mask and helmet when I felt the first blast of water.

It threw me back against a tree by the truck, and I held on to the tree with my eyes and mouth closed.

The force of the water was like a million needles on my skin. It was cold but felt wonderful. I was tempted to open my mouth a bit so I could drink some water, but I didn't.

The water pressure lessened, and I was being turned, my arms held out, and I let whoever it was lead me.

The water stopped, and I wiped my eyes so I could open them and see.

Blinking, I was surprised to see a ring of fire fighters shielding me from prying eyes. Their backs to me facing and outward. I shook my head and water came off me like a dog shaking after a swim. I reached up and squeezed out my hair.

Only then did I realize I was standing on the sidewalk, next to a tree dripping wet and wearing nothing but my hot-pink lacy bra and panty set.

I gasped and took the blanket Nancy held out for me. I pulled it around my shoulders, now completely over-whelmed how the day was ending.

"It's not every day we have to hose someone down wearing sexy lingerie. I like your style," she said with a grin.

Chapter Eight

Are you as good as you think you are?

Chapter Nine

Taylor held his phone in his palm and looked at Drea's number on the screen. It was time they talked. They'd be working together on cases, and he didn't want any awkwardness between them. He'd sensed her hesitancy, and there was really no need for it.

They were both professionals and would behave as such, but they did need to have a conversation.

He still had a hard time believing she was here. Not in a million years did he ever think they'd see each other again.

After their weekend together, where it was agreed, what happens in Denver stays in Denver.

But he couldn't get her out of his head. About six months after the conference, unable to resist it any longer, he'd tried to find her. He didn't know her last name, nor she his, which definitely didn't help. Disappointed at his lack of success, Taylor kept his eyes open and hoped that one day they would stumble across each other again. And they had.

He'd been floored that day at the fatal fire when she'd turned around. As if punched in the gut, he'd done his best not to look like a stunned idiot. It was the absolute last thing

Taylor had expected, and she'd appeared just as startled. He'd followed her lead by pretending not to know each other.

Now, more than a few weeks later, she'd been on his mind constantly and he still couldn't shake the fact she had moved to Oak Creek. Bringing their long-ago weekend together blasting back into reality. Had fate decided to step in and give them another chance?

It wasn't only their sexual chemistry that was over the top. It was the other facets of their weekend. The peace, comfort, conversations, and quiet moments saying absolutely nothing.

They hadn't touched on anything to suggest long term, but he'd felt something shift inside him. And he was pretty sure she'd felt it too. They'd said their goodbyes and gone off in opposite directions.

Years had gone by, and Taylor had never forgotten her. He'd often wondered what if? What if they'd stayed in contact? What if they hadn't said what happens in Denver stays in Denver.

He drew in a breath and sent her a text.

Meet for coffee?

There. Done. And now he'd wait for a reply. Not expecting one to come back right away, he put his phone back in his pocket and continued to sign off on the reports.

His phone buzzed, and he was pleasantly surprised to see it was her. It hadn't taken that long for her to reply.

A good sign?

Sure, when you free?

He checked his watch and started typing a message back.

I'll be on the road at two thirty, somewhere around then? Will that work?"

Yeah, I should be good. Same place?

Yes, are you at a scene?

I'm finishing up what was rather a dramatic event. I can tell you about it later.

Taylor liked how the conversation seemed normal. Easy. Like they were old friends. Just like how they'd conversed when they first met. His heart skipped a beat, and he smiled. He wasn't a schoolboy, but he sure did feel happy knowing he'd see Drea later.

* * *

Taylor was in the lot, and he didn't see her truck, so he decided to wait in the car and review one of the intern's reports. He rolled the windows down and a nice breeze blew through. It was getting hot again.

"Hey there."

Taylor was startled by Drea's voice.

"Hey." He put the files down and closed the windows.

He got out of the car, and they fell into step walking quietly to the coffee shop. He pulled open the door. "After you."

She smiled and entered. She was wearing her work clothes, cargo pants and a logoed T-shirt tucked in, kept snug with a leather belt. Her solid black leather boots increased her height a bit, but she still had to look up to him.

The simple and efficient outfit did little to hide her sexuality. She looked damn hot, and he appreciated the view. Her easy gait made her hips swing, and memories of them together flashed in his mind.

"It was nice to hear from you." Drea stopped at the end of the line, crossed her arms, and faced him.

"I was thinking maybe we should get together and talk."

She nodded, and they shuffled forward as the line moved. "I was thinking the same thing."

Her gaze caught his, and they stared at each other. A small smile curved her lips, and he wondered what she was thinking.

Remembering the weekend? He wondered if it was on her mind as much as it was on his.

With drinks in hand, they found a seat outside in the shade. Taylor would rather be away from any eaves-droppers.

"It's been what, five years since Denver?" He sat opposite her.

"Yes, hard to believe. Seems like yesterday, and yet also eons ago." She settled and put her cup on the table.

"I did try to find you about six months later, but you'd moved on," he told her.

"You did? I wish I'd known." She sipped her iced coffee and looked pensive. "I've never been one to stay in one place for long. I live a rather nomadic lifestyle, which also helps with experience. I go where the work needs me."

Their gazes met, and he searched hers to see if there was anything there. A connection. A spark.

He wasn't sure, but he thought he saw something lurking in the gray depths.

"I hear you've had a bit of trouble," he commented, hoping she would tell him what's going on.

Drea put her cup down. "It's probably nothing. But I had to report a slashed tire to the police since it was the company vehicle that was damaged. I don't understand some people."

"I agree. Has anything else happened?" Taylor felt protective toward her, and he wanted her to know he was here if she needed him.

She lifted a shoulder and gazed off to her vehicle, then she looked back at him. "A note or two."

"Note? What kind of note?" This alarmed him.

"It's dumb really. Just insensible words that I'm choosing not to take as a threat." She lifted her cup and took a sip, then startled almost spilling her drink when a car blasted its horn and tires screeched.

She was jumpy. So no, she was more concerned than she was letting on. He sat back in the chair. "Is that the right thing to do? Did you report them to the police?"

"Just the first note. Shannon intervened on that one. Not the second." She looked uncomfortable.

"You've had two notes? When did you get the second one?" This wasn't good.

"It was in the mail at the office." Drea looked into her cup, and didn't make eye contact with him.

"Could you tell if it came internally or externally?

She met his gaze finally, and shook her head. "It just had my name on the envelope." She paused a beat. "Do you think I should file a report?"

"Yes, actually, I do. You've had two notes, your truck was vandalized and that's a lot in a short space of time. It seemed targeted to me. I don't want to frighten you, but –

"Well you have," she said in a low voice and then

rushed the next words, "what I mean is, well ... I filed a report."

It was clear she was trying hard to be chill about the notes, but she wasn't doing a very good job. She glanced around nervously, as if looking for something to happen.

Taylor reached across the table and rested his hand on hers. "Look, I'm here, okay. I'd be happy to come to the police station with you or sit by you when you call."

When she met his gaze, he saw the concern I in them and the urge to comfort her overwhelmed him.

"Thank you. It's strange that I've come to a new town, not knowing anyone here, and we've stumbled across each other." She smiled, effectively changing the subject. But he decided he wouldn't let it go that easily. This could be a dangerous situation.

"I was thinking the same thing. Like it's meant to be." He wanted to keep their conversation lighthearted under the current circumstances. "Look, we had a fantastic weekend together." He gave her a cheeky smile and was pleased when she laughed.

"Didn't we though? So I guess we're not really strangers."

"I hardly think so." He finished his coffee and allowed her to steer the conversation.

"Have you been in Oak Creek long?"

"I came about a year after Denver."

"During the pand –

"Yes." He rushed the word. "There was a need here."

She nodded and cast her eyes down. He felt bad at the way he snapped.

"And you? What brought you here," he asked wanting to divert the topic of conversation.

She looked at him. "Shannon told me about the opening, and I felt like it was time for a change."

"Do you move around a lot?"

"I have been. It's hard for me to stay in one."

Taylor wondered if there was a reason she moved about, likely there was and maybe she'd tell him. "Well, I hope you stay here for a while." He smiled, as did she.

"We'll see."

He was disappointed at her reply. Taylor was hoping to hear she would give Oak Creek a chance. That would mean they may be able to rekindle what they had in Denver.

* * *

They sat in the shade chatting about life, the town, their jobs, but they both seemed to carefully stay away from any deeper, more intimate conversation.

Taylor watched her eyes dart around, and he knew she was more unnerved by the incidents since she'd arrived than she wanted to let on.

She was alone in a new town, with a new job, living in a hotel. She didn't know anyone really. He felt for her.

"Why don't you move in with me for a while?" The words tumbled out and he was surprised when he heard them.

Her head snapped around, and she looked at him with eyebrows raised, and a stunned expression on her face. "Excuse me? What?"

She shifted in the chair. He knew he'd just dropped a bomb on her, and him, if truth be told. It may be uncomfortable and sudden, but it made perfect sense.

"Sure, I mean, you can bring Cinder. It's a safe place. You won't have to worry about this stalker person. I have the room. Between my job and yours, we may never be in the house at the same time."

He paused and wondered what was racing around in her brain. Because his was doing backflips thinking of all the ways it could and may not work.

"It makes sense, don't you think?" He lifted his shoulders.

She chewed her lip and fiddled with the now-empty cup. She was slightly nodding her head, and he could almost hear her brain clicking through all the scenarios. He felt a tiny burst of encouragement.

"But why would you do this?" Her vulnerability when she said the words hit him square in the chest.

He reached across and touched her fingers. "No pressure, Drea. It's simply a suggestion that could be the answer for you right now. My house is big, and I don't have a cat." He smiled at her, and she returned it. "I'd like the company. To know someone else is living there with me. To make the house feel full."

He fell silent and thought about his words. They were raw, and truthful. It was the first time he'd ever worded how he really felt. It was a hard realization.

He was lonely too. He was alone. He was empty. They were two people that could find solace in each other's company.

"Way to turn on the guilt," she said with a smile.

He laughed to cover up the moment of his own vulnerability. "Did it work?"

She narrowed her eyes and tried to hold back a grin. "Strictly for convenience. No funny business."

Taylor chuckled. "Funny business? That is a pretty broad description. I think you might have to narrow it down a little."

She smiled, and the way her face lit up was like a reward.

"It's settled then. Do you want to move in tonight or tomorrow?"

"Uhm, it's getting late now, and I've paid for tonight. So how about tomorrow morning? What time do you leave for work?"

"Hang on." Taylor pulled out his phone and checked the morning schedule. "I have a PM at eleven. So any time before ten thirty."

"Okay, I'll get there by nine thirty. I'm seeing Shannon this evening before she's off again, so I can pack after, get Cinder first thing, and head over."

"Great, I'll text you my address." He was pleased she'd agreed to come and stay with him. Of course, he couldn't help thinking about their last time together. But that's not what this is about. This is about somebody needing a hand, and he was able to offer it.

He stood as did she, and she placed her hand on his arm. Yes, they definitely still had that electric connection.

"Taylor." Her voice was low, and he turned to her. "Thank you. I really do appreciate it." She pressed her lips together and gave him a slight nod.

"You're welcome. I'm happy to help."

He walked her to her truck.

"I'll have a storage unit ready for my stuff, and my SUV is being shipped as well. When it arrives, is it okay for two vehicles in your driveway?"

"Of course it is, and you don't need storage. Have it all sent to my place."

He opened the truck door for her.

"It's a not a lot. Some furniture and boxes that I've kept

over the years. I can put it in storage until I find my own place."

His heart dropped, and he didn't want to show disappointment that she was thinking their living arrangement was temporary. He hadn't really thought that far ahead.

"I have a large garage on the property that will be able to store it all."

She looked up at him, and they gazed into each other's eyes. He wanted to take her by the shoulders and pull her in for a kiss. If he did that, he'd be stepping over an undrawn line. So when she leaned in to give him a hug, he couldn't have been more surprised.

Taylor slowly tightened his hold on her and inhaled her soft scent. He was elated when she gripped him. They stood like that for the longest moment and let each other go at the same time.

"See you tomorrow then," she said and climbed into her vehicle.

"Yes. I'll have coffee."

Drea laughed. "Good, I need my coffee!"

Chapter Ten

I'm going to show you you're not as good as you think
you are.

Chapter Eleven

I cupped the glass of bourbon between my palms and looked over my shoulder at the door. I was waiting for Shannon. We'd arranged to meet up and have a bite to eat before she had to head out to another case. The place was packed, and I was lucky to snag two stools at the bar.

Taylor's suggestion of moving in with him had caught me by complete surprise. It was obvious our chemistry was still lit. I mean, whenever I was around him, I was hard pressed to not get all jittery and aroused.

Our weekend wasn't easily forgettable. Before stumbling across each other here in Oak Creek, I'd held on to our time together as a wonderful memory to cherish. Something to remember when I was older and that part of my life had faded away. I didn't want to admit how sad that made me. To not have a physical and emotional relationship as I aged actually broke my heart.

And then boom, here he was in the flesh. A hot memory sprung to life, and one I realized I wanted to relive again.

And again.

So why did I find it hard to look him in the eye, to let him stand close to me? How was it possible I felt shy?

Shy!

Seriously, what we had done together was far from vanilla, so to feel shy was ridiculous. Even now, my heart skipped a beat thinking about him, and I gripped the glass when I swayed, feeling lightheaded.

I took another drink of the bourbon. It seared my throat and warmed my belly. But it did not ease the growing ache for him. Suddenly, I was warm. I wish I could rip off my clothes and cool down. Taking another drink only accomplished raising my body heat even more.

And his offer to move in with him! It was a whole other matter I struggled to make sense of. Even though I'd already accepted his offer, I questioned if it really was a good idea. The thought of us sleeping under the same roof, in different bedrooms just down the hall from each other, seemed very dangerous indeed.

How long would it be before we found our way into the same bed? Goosebumps rippled along my arms. I was pretty sure it wouldn't take long. I'd been celibate for a while, and I'd finally accepted that our Denver tryst had ruined me for other men. Nothing compared.

I finished the remainder of the alcohol and welcomed the fiery heat as I allowed myself to imagine us together again.

Erotic thoughts aside, if I was honest with myself, moving in with Tayler did make sense. My vehicle would be safe parked in his driveway. I wouldn't be alone in case of any further threats. Not that I needed to have someone close by to keep me safe, I told myself, but it did ease my mind a bit.

I picked at the coaster under the glass, replaying the

other notes that had been left for me. The one on the truck. In the mail at the office, and front desk of the hotel.

Just thinking about them made me shiver and my scalp prickle. I gritted my teeth, knowing I couldn't let this escalate. It could jeopardize my career and emotional well-being. I'd given the notes to the police, so it was in their hands. They didn't really make sense either. I finished the drink in a gulp.

I thought back over a lot of my cases. I'd been an expert witness in court providing evidence. Most of the people I'd testified against had been found guilty of arson and incarcerated. One guy had taken a couple of years to nail, but he'd ended up with nine years.

He went after abandoned buildings, some historical, which was a shame, because their beautiful architecture had been gutted by fire. It broke my heart to see the charred buildings that had once held life. But at least no one had been hurt or died in those fires. The guy was a creep and had stared me down when he was led from the courtroom. He'd made a gesture with his hands that he'd be watching me. I faced him down, and he'd turned away first. But it had shaken me.

Part of the decision to move away from my last job was the fire in my complex that had engulfed my work truck in the garage. I couldn't prove it was deliberate, but my gut told me otherwise. It certainly was ironic to see a fire investigator's burned-out work truck.

There had been an investigation, one I couldn't be part of, and it had been deemed non-suspicious.

That didn't sit right with me. I'd mentioned my concern, but there had been no evidence of wrongdoing and the case had been closed. But now, thinking about the sketchy things happening since I'd arrived here, I wondered if they were connected.

That led me back to that one arsonist we'd finally caught after two years and multiple fires. He'd been a bit scary, the way he stared at me in court, and I'd shook it off. How could he be responsible? He was in jail. I shivered thinking that it was possible he could somehow reach me from behind the bars of his cell.

Pub sounds invaded my thoughts. I glanced at the door and then at the crowd of people around me. If I ended up staying here, I'd get to know a lot of them, and they'd get to know me. So far, everyone I'd met had been great. Well, except for the person that had slashed my tires.

"Penny for your thoughts." I spun around to see who had crept up on me. Damn. I'm jumpy. It was the firefighter I'd seen at Kali's.

"Oh, hey. How are you?"

"Good. We have to stop meeting in restaurants. Did you enjoy the rest of your breakfast?"

"I did, thanks."

He lifted my bag off the stool and put it on the bar as he slid in beside me. I frowned.

"I'm, ah, waiting for someone."

A look flashed across his face before he masked it. "The more the merrier." His smile seemed just a bit too wide.

"Well, actually, no," I answered. "Girls' night, you know how it is. Sorry."

"Sure. I'll keep you company and then mosey off when your friend arrives."

But I don't want you too. I drew in a breath and cast about for something to say.

"Did you start firefighting in Oak Creek?" I asked as I swirled my glass, and the ice cubes clinked.

He took a drink from his beer and then shook his head. "No and yes. I came out as a fire jumper a few years ago during the wildfires, and then sort of drifted here. It was an unexpected place to land, but I like it."

"Seems like a nice place."

"How did you end up here?" he asked.

It was an innocent enough question, and I almost answered it. His expression held anticipation, and I felt a prickle along my spine.

"Nothing as exciting as your reason." I shrugged. "Just a job opening."

I wish Shannon would hurry up. This guy was giving me the heebie-jeebies.

"Girl on Fire" by Alicia Keyes came on the jukebox.

"Hey, that's you," he said.

"What?" I spun to look at him.

"The song." He tipped the neck of his beer bottle toward the jukebox. "'Girl on Fire'. That's you."

"No, it's not."

"Sure it is—"

"Hey, I see you didn't wait for me." Shannon nudged me from behind and raised her finger to the bartender.

"About time. Sit, sit," I told her and then looked at the guy whos name I still didn't know. "My friend is here." I hoped he'd take the hint.

He slowly stood, his eyes shifting between Shannon and me. Yeah, the sooner he's gone the better.

She looked at him with a smile and then dismissed him by seating herself and focusing on me.

"You're late." I lifted my glass and took a sip, giving her a look. Over her shoulder, I watched the guy walk away.

"I know, sorry. I got tied up. I was hoping to stay for another few days, but I actually have to go tomorrow.

There's another case, and it's a long drive. Flying will be too much of a headache because of all my crap I need to— Hey, what's wrong? You haven't heard a word I said."

"I'm sorry. That guy just creeped me out. I'm glad you came when you did."

"What guy?" She looked over her shoulder. "Oh, him." She waved her hand. "He's harmless, a local firefighter."

"You know him?"

"No, but I've seen him around." She pulled the cocktail napkin closer to her. "He's kind of a clinger-oner, but for some reason, he doesn't blend well with the crew but he tries."

I looked over at him and found he was watching me. What the hell?

I swiveled my gaze back to Shannon. "Oh, okay. So no need to worry about him then? Even though I feel like he's stalking me?"

"No, but why would you think you need to worry about him?" she asked, took a drink, and then her mouth shaped like an O. "The notes, tires... I get it." She shook her head. "Why would he do anything like that? He's been here for a while, so we'd have seen signs of it before now. I'm confident he is not your guy. Did you get another one?"

"Why does anyone do anything? People can be deceptive. Anyway, that makes me feel a bit better. Sorta." I nodded. "And yeah, I did, and before you jump all over me, yes, the cops have it."

"Good, and why only sorta?" She sipped from the straw of her fancy cocktail.

"Because that means he's ruled out." I tipped my head in the dude's direction. "Which means the culprit sending me notes is still out there." I picked up the menu.

"Ah, yeah, I get it. Just watch your back, huh? I don't want anything happening to you."

"You and me both." I lifted my glass, and we clinked.

We decided to get a few appetizers and split them since we couldn't decide on a dinner plate.

A conversation behind me drifted into my awareness when I heard Taylor's name. My ears perked up. I tried to listen and tune out all the other bar noise so I could hear what they were saying.

I leaned back on the barstool, hoping not to appear too obvious I was eavesdropping.

Taylor?

Yeah, was an ER doc. Good-looking guy too. I wonder if he's single—

Chair legs scraping on the floor drowned out the next few words. I made a tsk sound and turned my head in order to hear better.

Someone died and he took blame. Killed...

My heart leapt out of my chest. What the hell.

No, nothing like that. It was—

There were more bar noises, and chills ran down my spine. What happened to him? Why was he blamed, did he kill someone?

Changed to coroner.

It dawned on me then. Something had happened, and he'd felt responsible. I closed my eyes, remembering what I'd said to him the first time we saw each other at the fire scene.

"I'm the coroner."

"Coroner? You're a doctor."

"I am a doctor." He'd stiffened and a tight expression had crossed his face.

"Yes, I know, but a doctor doctor."

"Shit," I said under my breath and looked down at the menu.

"Hey, what's wrong?" Shannon asked, suddenly alert and looking around. "That's the second time you've scared the crap outta me."

"Sorry." I patted her hand. "I was just thinking of something I said to someone."

"To who? What did you say?" Her eyes showed concern. "Tell me, maybe it'll make you feel better."

"Taylor."

Her eyebrows shot up. "Taylor? What about him?"

I was silent for a beat and took the moment to gulp a few big drinks of my fancy cocktail. I sucked in a breath at the heat flaming down my throat.

"I said something to him at the fatal fire scene my first day that may have been insensitive." I glanced at her.

"What on earth could you say that would be insensitive? You don't even know him." She swung on the stool, and her knees touched my thigh. She covered my hand with hers. "It's okay. You can tell me."

I looked around to see if anyone was paying us any mind. Maybe I could just give her the barest details and she wouldn't overreact.

"We've met before—

"What!?" she all but screeched.

Nope no chance of her not overreacting.

"Shh! Come on, be quiet," I whisper shouted.

"Oops, sorry." She lowered her voice and leaned closer. "Tell me more."

I drew in a big breath and let it out slowly, tapping my fingers on the surface of the bar. "We met a few years ago at a conference." I gave her a sideways glance.

She gasped, and her eyebrows climbed up her forehead. She looked like a surprised fish, and I laughed.

"You did not! Was it dirty? Was it fun? Was it more than once?" she asked. "I want details!"

"All of the above," I said in a low voice, feeling my face heat up.

"Oh my God. Why did you never tell me? This is huge!"

"Because it was just a weekend. We agreed that's all it would be. No entanglements and no promises. We didn't even exchange phone numbers, and we only ever knew each other's first names. It was all very one-night standish."

"I'm speechless." Then she burst out laughing. "And you know me, speechless—" she pointed at herself, "—is relatively rare."

I nodded and smiled. "Oh ya, I definitely know that." I fell silent and gazed at the bottles lining the wall behind the bartender. I did feel a little bit better for telling her and getting it off my chest. But I was still conflicted on the other thing bothering me.

"What else? Something else is bugging you." She nudged my arm. "Come on, spill it."

"Not sure you're ready for this one." I sucked in a breath, widened my eyes, and looked at her. "He asked me to move in with him."

This time, her screech was earsplitting enough to shatter glasses and booze bottles. She did accomplish silencing Hooligans though, and for a quiet beat, everyone looked around for the source of the scream and then promptly picked up their conversations again.

"Stop that! You can't shriek every time I say something."

"But the things you are telling me are totally shriek worthy! Alright now, back up and tell me how this came about."

The artichoke dip, mozzarella sticks, hot wings, potato skins and pitcher of beer we ordered was placed before us.

"Whoa, that's a lot of food," I said and grabbed a mozz stick.

"Whatever, we can ask for a doggie bag. I'm waiting to hear...all of it."

I reached for a crispy bit of naan and dragged it through the dip. I told her about our conversation in between eating. I was starved and paused sucking up the rest of my cocktail.

"Aww, how sweet of him to ask you to move in with him." She nodded and gave me a few winks.

"Yeah, okay, but it's not really for that. Of course, it will be hard to not think about that, because gawd, it was hot. I do think I will feel better living with someone else. I could potentially have a stalker and it makes sense not to be alone."

"Abso-freaking-lutley. It's awful what has been happening. I'm so sorry. And I agree, it's good to have someone else nearby. When do you move in?"

"I'll pack up tonight, grab the cat, and go over about nine thirty tomorrow. He has a PM at eleven."

"This is moving quickly. Nice, very nice." Shannon was totally into this, and her excitement evident. It actually eased my concerns and made me think all would be okay.

For the first time in a while, I began to feel relaxed. As if I'd been holding my breath forever and able to finally let it out. Could be the drinks too, taking the edge of things. I looked at Shannon. I was glad we were friends and had made this evening happen before she had to take off.

During the next couple of hours, we munched, chatted, and laughed, but the way I'd spoken to Taylor on that first day was never far from my thoughts. I would have to do right by that.

And I hoped he would tell me his story in his own time.

Chapter Twelve

"*Why don't you move in with me?*"

I replayed Taylor's words over and over. I'd been floored by his offer. It had come out of the blue.

I'd been a hard sell, and it had been difficult to find a reason to turn him down.

It wouldn't be for long, I told myself. Just until I could get things organized and make sure I would be staying put.

I shivered, and it wasn't from being cold. How long would we be sleeping in our own rooms, in our own beds, knowing the other was just down the hall?

Sharing a bed with Taylor was tantalizing for sure... knowing we would be doing more than sleeping. My body remembered his touch. The brush of his lips on my skin, the strength—and gentleness—of his fingers on me...in me. I drew in a ragged breath and welcomed the air blowing in the truck window. Something had to cool my heated blood.

It astounded me that all these years later, our paths had crossed and everything we'd shared that weekend had come back with a vengeance.

I shifted in my seat, still unsure I was making the right decision. If only I could put out the fire fanning through my body. Living in a state of arousal whenever I thought of Taylor or whenever he was close by, couldn't be good. Could it?

I stuck my arm out the window and let my hand ride on the air. I'd do this as a kid to distract myself on long drives, only now I was doing it to temper the heat rising in me.

Shannon thought moving in with him was a good idea and had done her best to convince me. Taylor had also pushed home the point it would be safer. I could bring Cinder too. Maybe they were working in cahoots with each other.

I had to admit, both were valid reasons. It wouldn't be forever either. It was a stopgap to get me out of the hotel. Of course, I'd filed a report with the police about the harassment. I didn't think there was much they could do about it, not unless the person grew bolder, which I hoped they wouldn't.

Cinder meowed, and I pressed my fingertips to the door of his carrier, stroking his now soft and clean hair.

"Not long now, baby."

Between both of our jobs, the chances of Taylor and I being in the house at the same time could be minimal.

The sun flickered through the leaves giving a lovely morning light as I drove down the street watching for my turn. With the window open, the cab filled with the scent of freshly mowed lawn and flowers. I loved summer. It was just so wonderfully perfect.

The scent of the grass threw me back to my childhood. Before the fire that had ruined everything. It was probably one of the last times I'd ever felt safe or happy.

I inhaled a deep breath and held it for a moment before

letting it out nice and slow. It wasn't often I felt this light, with the weight of the pressures momentarily forgotten. It was difficult to hold on to the calm and contented feeling that filled the emptiness inside me.

I turned at the next stop sign. The trees were bigger, the yards wider, the homes older, and I think I fell in love. This neighborhood was lovely and perfect for raising a family. My heart pinched.

Perhaps one day. I shook it off and watched carefully for the next turn. We'd agreed this arrangement was strictly for convenience. Were we friends? Maybe colleagues. I couldn't quite put my finger on what we were. Previous fuck buddies?

I cringed. That was kind of hard, but it was the truth. Right?

Dwelling on our pact wouldn't do any good, especially since we'd both agreed it was not too bad we'd bumped into each other. All we could do was to give it a go and see how things played out. Could we go from lovers, separation, to friends, and back to lovers?

But damn! Now all I could think of was our how we reconnected, and the connection we obviously still had. The memories of our weekend blended with our recent encounters and I knew it would be impossible to put them back in Pandora's box.

Damn, Pandora and her box anyway!

The GPS voiced my next turn.

The final turn.

I reminded myself I knew absolutely nothing about him, nor did he know anything about me. But what I did know was how excellent we were in bed together. I also knew he had a caring side. He had offered his place. I couldn't forget what I'd overheard though...that he'd potentially killed someone.

I drew in a shaky breath and leaned forward, watching for his driveway and giving myself a stern talking to that I could do this. It would be fine.

Cinder let out a long yowl.

I stuck my finger through the door on the cat carrier. He nudged it, and I glanced at him. His beautiful eyes watched me. He was a very rare and loving cat. I was glad he'd picked me.

"We're almost there, and then you have the run of the place." I turned my attention back to the street when the GPS announced I'd arrived at my destination.

I was pleasantly surprised. I hadn't really known what to expect, but it definitely hadn't been this. As I drove into his driveway, I couldn't shake the feeling like I was coming home.

Taylor met Drea in the driveway. He was looking forward to their new arrangement.

He grabbed two of her duffle bags and a leather satchel while she got a few other smaller bags and the cat carrier.

"Come on in. Let's get you and Cinder settled and take your bags up to your room."

Taylor led the way, fully aware of her behind him. He'd been worried about this change since he'd blurted out his offer yesterday without any forethought.

Spontaneity wasn't in his character, so he'd surprised himself and her as well He'd been so careful to keep his emotions in check and remain distant after the death of his sister-in-law that he'd had a difficult time bouncing back from.

Deep down he still felt he'd failed people, and the results of that had been far-reaching. It had shaken his confidence, and it wasn't easy to overcome feeling inadequate. It had estranged him from his brother. He could only hope one day they would be able to mend their relationship.

The result was Taylor never wanted it to happen again, or to be responsible for someone else, and yet, here he was, helping someone in need.

He'd been concerned for Drea, though. The kind of intimacy they'd shared in Denver wasn't easy to forget.

He put her bags down.

"Should I let him out here?" Taylor asked.

"I should put his litter somewhere and show it to him. Where is best?" Drea held up shopping bags.

"How about in the laundry room? It's off the mudroom at the back of the kitchen."

"Sounds good."

He led the way, and they got the litter pan ready.

"Okay buddy, welcome to your new home," Taylor told Cinder and opened the door to the carrier.

He bolted out and slid to a stop with his tail puffed out ears up and twitching as he looked around with his wide eyes.

They laughed.

"Hey, boy, it's okay. Get used to your new home." Drea picked him up and carried him to the laundry room, showing him his private facilities.

Taylor watched her with the cat, and he already felt optimistic. Life was in the house and it seemed full. Just as he'd hoped. He was positive they'd make it work, the living-together part anyway. The sexual side might be a bit more challenging.

"Let's get your bags up to your room. I'm going to have to leave soon, and I want to show you around."

"Please, don't worry about me. I'll figure everything out if you have to go. Thanks again for this offer. It's really great of you."

The look in her eye actually made his heart beat double time. It wasn't the same fiery expression from their weekend, it was different. A softness, gratitude and something else that lingered for only a moment.

"It's my pleasure. I'm glad to be able to help out." He glanced over his shoulder as he mounted the stairs. Her hand slid up the wooden banister, fingers gently curved as she watched her footing on the steps. Cinder barreled past them, roared down the hall, and skidded to a stop.

"He's going to be a character." Taylor turned and waited for her at the top of the stairs.

"He is cute, and I'm sure he'll settle down soon. At least I hope so."

She glanced up at him, and he sucked in a quiet breath when their gazes met.

Yep, the connection was still there, and like spontaneous combustion, it had sparked to life with no help. They both froze, she on the top step and him on the landing. The quiet of the house wrapped around them, and he just looked into her gray eyes. They were clear and soft, and he was reminded of the stormy, sultry depths that had filled them on their weekend.

She cleared her throat and took the final step to the landing, stopping in front of him. Very close.

"This is a lovely old house." She pulled her gaze from him and looked down the upstairs hall. "It's so bright and cheery."

"Thanks. I like it. I was lucky when it came on the market and snatched it up. It is a bit big, but you never know what you will grow into, right?" He glanced at her and smiled.

She looked up and nodded. "So true. Maybe one day kids will be racing up and down the stairs instead of a cat."

"That would be nice." He heard a tone in her voice, almost wistful. Was she also hoping for that in her future?

Taylor couldn't imagine going through life without children, a wife, a family to love and care for, but caring is the reason he skirted any relationship entanglements.

He was a doctor. And he'd been unable to save the sick and had to remember, he wasn't the only medical professional that faced the pandemic and all the tragedy. Taylor walked through a door and over to the window.

"This is it. The room overlooks the back garden. It's quiet, and the tree fills with birds. Which can be annoying if you want to sleep in." He pushed back the curtain a little more so she could see out.

"Oh my gosh. It's beautiful and huge." She put her bag on the bed and gazed around then turned to him.

Her smile was wide, and the delight on her face chased away any second thoughts he may have of her moving in. It was going to work.

"This should be your room. It's your house, and it's far too grand for me."

"It's perfect for you. I'm pleased you're happy." He smiled, glad she liked the room.

She nodded. "Yes, thank you. I'm worried I'll like it too much and not want to leave."

Taylor realized in that instant he didn't want her to leave either. He wanted the company, to have her stay with him. And just maybe—

He stopped himself. That kind of thinking would ruin him. He did his best to keep the smile on his face, even if it had brought reality back like a punch in the gut.

Of course, she wouldn't stay long. How could he even have considered it? But his reaction when she said it surprised him.

Thoughts to ponder. He hadn't realized he was lonely until she was here standing in a bedroom in his house which was actually the primary bedroom. A bedroom that should have a couple in it...

"Don't worry. I'm fine. My room is plenty big enough." He pointed down the hall. "It's at the front of the house. My office is in between, and there's another small bedroom on the other side of the stairs if you'd like to use it as an office."

The center staircase rose up in the middle of the second floor onto a landing that ringed the stairs with access to all the rooms with a waist-high wooden railing around the landing offering a view of the entrance below.

"Your room has an en-suite bathroom. There's another full bathroom just in there." He pointed to the other side of the landing beside the smaller bedroom.

"This really is something." She rested her hands on the honey-colored wood railing and looked over. "I love this balcony around the stairs and the rooms on each side."

Taylor smiled, happy she liked his home. "It's one of the features that I really liked when I originally found it."

"Anyone would be pleased to live in such a gracious home."

He liked that she said home and not house. Because home meant so much more to him.

"Now, how about we get you and Cinder all settled."

"Sounds like a plan. I never know when I'm going to get called out." She turned, and they were face-to-face.

So close that all he had to do was reach out and snag her waist. He ached to have her next to him again. Their bodies pressed tightly together from shoulder to hip, her arms around his neck, thighs pressed to his. He bit back a groan as they stared at each other for a beat.

Drea lifted her hand and then hesitated, looking up into his eyes.

"Very true." His voice a low rumble. "I'm always waiting for that call as well."

Drea captured him with those wonderful eyes, and he hardly registered anything else except the two of them.

"Imagine this," she whispered. "Us. Bumping into each other all these years later."

"Yes, imagine that." Taylor couldn't look away from her, and he almost reached for her with the overpowering urge to kiss her senseless.

***

I could have swooned like a virgin. The look in Taylor's eyes burned into my soul. I knew what he wanted, and if I was honest with myself, oh, how I wanted him as well.

We'd been dancing around this for days. It was bound to come to a head, and it was quite ridiculous to think we could avoid the past.

I'm sure he remembered as well as I did the chemistry we'd shared. I felt it now, as I'm sure he did. There really wasn't a way to avoid falling into each other's arms again. Or any way we could not want a taste of what we had before.

That one taste was unforgettable.

I let out a breath. Oh, the hell with it. I reached up and took his face in my hands, rubbing my thumb across his lips.

He blinked with surprise and then his expression changed to one I remembered so well. From ... *before*

I gasped when his arms whipped around my waist, and he hauled me against him. It happened so fast I had no time to collect my thoughts.

I didn't care. We stood at the top step entwined and tottering precariously close to the edge. The warmth of his body wrapped around me, and our eyes were pinned on each other. Pushing my fingers through his close-cropped dark hair now speckled with a little gray, I reveled in the velvety feel of it. The spicy scent of his maleness was exactly the right combination of pheromones to ignite me.

I wanted him. Badly. My blood was superheated, and I sucked in a deep breath. Like a backdraft, I was about to combust.

He raised his eyebrows, and I nodded. In the next moment, we were intertwined as one. His lips on mine, his tongue delving into my mouth, and mine finding his.

We were frantic. Wild. Every atom in my body came alive. Fleeting images of our first time together filled my mind. His arousal against my belly was my undoing. I ran my hands down his back, loving the feel of his corded muscles. Gripping his ass, I pushed my hips into him, needing to feel him next to me.

All sounds were drowned out except the breathlessness of our passion. He backed me up, bracing me between him and the wall. The bed was only steps away, but we made no move to it.

We pulled at our clothing, and his shirt was soon off. I struggled with mine. He pushed my hands away, his mouth still on mine as he slid his hands underneath, his palms flat against my skin until he cradled my breasts in his hands.

I sighed, sagging against the wall, forcing him to shift

and hold me. My legs wouldn't work properly, and I clung to him, noticing the new tattoos inked over his shoulders. I found them an amazing turn-on.

His lips found that spot on my neck he'd discovered before. It was magic. The slight stubble on his chin blended with the softness of his lips and his tongue, and I was done. His stubble rasped over my skin, and I didn't care if I was left with evidence showing on my neck and cheek.

Only with him had I ever been able to fully let myself feel. No barriers, no obstacles, no outside thoughts intruded into our inner world.

It was happening again, and I loved it.

"Oh my God, Taylor," I moaned and turned my face to his.

"Drea. Drea. I never thought we'd see each other again." His breath was warm on my flesh, and he worked his way to my mouth.

We fell into the kiss. Deep and tantalizing. I was lost in him. Absorbed in the moment, all sense of space and time, everything, faded except his touch.

He lifted his head and stared down at me, his chest heaving, and I blinked. His stormy-blue eyes were half closed, full of passion, and they made me gasp. I cupped his cheek.

"I k-know." I panted, trying to catch my breath. "That weekend. We said we'd always have Denver."

He nodded and pulled me into his arms. I wrapped mine around him. Desperation took hold of me and I held him tight. I couldn't get close enough to him.

How could we be here, was this going to be a complication we'd have to face?

"What are we going to do? I thought of you over the

years, but we made the agreement," I whispered into his shoulder, not really expecting an answer.

"We kept our agreement. A weekend together with no strings, but damn, it was hard to forget you. You have no idea how seeing you that first day at the fire affected me."

The one thing I remember about him was his succinct way of speaking.

Even though we were strangers in Denver and still are now, we weren't strangers when it came to sex. We didn't talk about our lives, likes, or dreams for the future. I knew my demons and was pretty sure he had some of his own. Like the reason he'd switched to be a medical examiner instead of a doctor. What had brought him to Oak Creek? What twist of fate had brought us back together?

Was great sex a solid enough foundation on which to build a relationship?

I was shocked that the idea of a relationship even crossed my mind. I was happy with my solitary life. At least, that's what I told myself. I was responsible only for me. Not reliant on anyone else, which was something I just couldn't bring myself to do. It was dangerous. People let you down.

When he stepped back, I grudgingly let him go, his shirt slipping through my fingers.

"Maybe we can simply enjoy each other," he suggested.

And there it was. The solution.

I nodded. "Yes, yes. I suppose."

It really wasn't an answer, but I didn't know what else to say. My phone buzzed in my bag on the bed I would soon be sleeping in. Would it work out, this cohabitation arrangement? Would we battle this sexual tension every day and night?

Was it sustainable?

Or would we succumb to it?

Could we become friends with benefits?

Who knew?

I fished my phone out of the bag and held it up. Taylor was standing in the doorway, his face unreadable. I mouthed work.

He nodded. I answered the call and then looked back at the door, but he was gone.

Chapter Thirteen

A lovely breeze blew in the bedroom windows. The curtains lifted and fluttered lazily. I snuggled into the soft sheets and watched them, mesmerized by their delicate dance. The pillows were perfectly plump and I couldn't be any more cozy. I could stay here all day.

My phone pinged and I picked it up, to see there was a storm advisory for later in the day.

Cinder was lying on the pillow next to me and looked at me with half closed eyes.

"I agree. Maybe a few more minutes then we can get up and make some coffee."

He stretched his paws out to me and I stroked his silky ear. We lay there for a while longer in the quiet house. I'd been here almost three weeks now and we were settling in quite well.

I'd not gotten any new notes since being here. Hopefully the person forgot about me, but I remained cautious.

"Okay buddy. Time to rise and shine."

I forced myself out of bed and went into the bathroom and came out a few moments later feeling more alive but still dragging my ass. Cinder still lay on the pillows and watched me get dressed.

"You can stay here as long as you want." I told him as I left the bedroom.

Taylor's bedroom door was closed, and I quietly went down the stairs with Cinder hot on my heels.

After making coffee, I put some ready-made dough for muffins in the oven. Then sat at the kitchen table with my phone beside the mug and Cinder curled up inside my arm with his back next to the warm cup. He was never far from my side when I was home.

Home.

I shook my head and smiled. It did feel like home, but I was cognizant of getting too comfortable. You never knew what would transpire and shake things upside down.

I absently stroked his head and twirled his ears while I scrolled through Insta. He moved onto his back, baring his belly. He was a real cute boy with a white spot on his chest and a lovely white heart on his belly. He was purring like an engine, loud and deep. He made me happy.

"I'm glad we found each other." I told him and he let out a quiet meow. I decided he agreed with me.

He'd adapted well to his new living arrangements. I had as well, but I was still acutely aware of the fact Taylor and I were under one roof. In separate bedrooms only a hall away.

We'd seen each other a few times since I moved in. It was a bit awkward after the kiss and all. Which, I couldn't forget by the way, and it was easy to let myself get lost in the fantasy of more happening between us. He was such a damn good kisser.

Today was the first time we were in the house all day together. I looked at the ceiling. Was he sleeping? Did he still sleep naked like he had in Denver? I closed my eyes and relived the image of him in my bed, the sheet slung low over his hips, his powerful chest tanned against the white sheets. My mouth went dry, and I picked up my mug. Cinder voiced his complaint.

"Sorry, bud, but I need this more than you." If my thoughts continued down that path, I was doomed.

Cinder rolled over and stretched. His paws flexed, showing his very impressive claws. I'd have to either take him back to Wags & Whiskers for a trim or figure out how to do it myself. I wonder how he would behave if I used nail clippers?

I took another drink of coffee and the lingering image of Taylor still forefront in my mind. I moaned in delight. Both were perfect. Hot, flavorful, and creamy. I blushed and then rubbed my cheeks. How dumb.

My phone pinged. I opened the notification app that advised crews of fire calls within the region. I didn't have to go to this one, thank goodness. I was looking forward to the weekend off and thought I might explore Oak Creek. I wanted to buy Cinder some toys, do some grocery shopping, and maybe bake some more. The muffins were starting to smell very yummy. I preferred making them from scratch, but the premix would do for now. I did feel a sense of obligation to contribute, it was only right, so I started a grocery list of what we needed.

Taylor's house was comfortable and a thousand times better than the hotel. I could definitely get used to living here.

The floor creaked above me, and my heart leapt into my throat. He was moving around and would probably come down soon. It would be the first morning he'd see me au natural, still bleary eyed, with messy hair and very slow moving. Not that I used a lot of cosmetics, but I hadn't even brushed my hair.

I forced myself to stay put and not jump up and check my look in the powder-room mirror. Instead, I focused on my phone, and held the mug to my mouth.

What did it matter how I looked anyway? But deep down, it did matter.

I heard his feet on the stairs, the front door open and then close.

"Morning, sunshine," he said brightly and tossed the newspaper on the table. "What is that delicious aroma I smell?"

Again, Cinder voiced his disapproval at the intrusion of the newspaper. Taylor rubbed his belly when he walked past to the coffee machine.

"Morning. There are muffins in the oven. You're chipper today." Even though I wanted to get things done, the thought of crawling back into bed for a little while was a sweet temptation.

"The sun is shining and it's a beautiful day," he replied, filling his mug.

"I remember now. You're a bright-eyed and bushy-tailed morning person." I groaned. He didn't reply, and I glanced at him from behind a hank of messy hair.

He raised his eyebrows and shook his head slightly.

"What?"

He lifted the mug to his mouth and watched me over the rim. "Ah, nectar of the gods. Nothing, it's just the first time you've referred to Denver."

"Oh really? I hadn't realized." I tried to be nonchalant about it, but Denver was always there, would always be there in the background and how we'd spent our weekend. The only time we'd talked about it was after the kiss. The memory of that kiss found its way into bed with me every night with my body wanting more.

"Do you have plans for today?" he asked.

"Other than just trying to discover a bit about the town, not really. I was going to go grocery shopping to help fill the pantry and fridge, but other than that, not really." I pushed my hair out of my face, and he watched my hand.

"How about you?" I asked him.

He shook his head. "Nothing in particular. I'd be happy to join you on your rounds and maybe show you a little bit more of the town."

I didn't even think twice. "Sure, that would be great." Obviously, my subconscious was working overtime.

Was it weird they were making arrangements for the day like an old married couple?

"Great, what time did you want to go?" He downed the rest of his coffee, took their mugs to the pot and refilled them.

"It doesn't really matter. Oh, could you take the muffins out please? I'm just looking forward to no deadlines, pressure, or expectations. Just going with the flow and letting it happen." I took the refilled cup from him. Nodding my thanks.

"I like that plan." Taylor placed his mug on the table and grabbed a tea towel took the hot muffin tin out of the oven. He put it on the stove, I watched him fish two out of the pan and put them on a plate. He came and sat across from me.

He must have remembered how I took my coffee from when we were at the coffee shop here or from Denver. Either way, I was impressed. Then I reminded myself I knew how he took his coffee as well. Did something as simple as how we take our coffee hold significance?

"Want any breakfast? I think I'll whip up some eggs," he asked and munched the top of a muffin.

"Sure, thank you. Don't go to any trouble, though." I reached for a muffin and pulled the top off to nibble.

"No trouble. Scrambled eggs and bacon was my plan." He finished the muffin and took his mug to the counter. I watched him move around the kitchen, heating the pan, getting the eggs and bacon from the fridge.

Soon, the aroma of bacon filled the air. He scrambled eggs and mixed in sharp cheddar cheese, making my mouth water. He placed the plate in front of me. It was garnished with a fruit kebab.

"Wow, this looks wonderful. I didn't know you're such a good cook." I lifted my fork, and he sat in front of me with his own plate.

"You never asked." He smiled around the bite of bacon.

"Maybe we just never had the time to discuss our lives." I paused with the fork midway to my mouth. Had I really just said that?

He laughed, and I joined in, easing the mood. And just like that, any tension I'd felt earlier was gone and I settled in to enjoy breakfast. Maybe we'd have a good day together.

"Well, I think I'll go and make myself look more presentable." I pushed back my chair.

"Don't feel you have to do that on my account. I think you look pretty damn nice just as you are."

Shivers of delight tingled along my arms, and I looked down at my oversized T-shirt and the black and white checked sleeping pants I had on.

"You need to get your eyes checked by a doctor," I told him when I rose and took our plates to the dishwasher.

He let out a burst of laughter. I tossed a dishtowel at

him and ran out of the kitchen laughing before he could retaliate. "I'll be back shortly"

"If you need any help, just holler," he called after me.

I nearly tripped on the step. Just call him if I needed help? I climbed the stairs wondering if he was teasing. He had to be, right? But after our kiss... I didn't know what to think.

I can't say I wasn't tempted to holler for him.

I peeled off my clothes after shutting the bedroom door and went into the en-suite. I stood in front of the mirror and gazed at myself. It was hard to look at myself without being judgmental. I saw a thirty-four almost thirty-five-year-old woman who was fit and muscled. My boobs were still good, and while I was glad for that, there was a side note of sadness, they hadn't nourished a baby.

I wanted to have a baby. It was a secret desire. I turned sideways and ran my hand down my belly, which was still flat from the fitness routine I followed and...no pregnancy.

One day.

I'd set a timeline. Actually, this was the year I was going to freeze some eggs. If no daddy-worthy man came along by the time I was thirty-six, I'd use them to have a baby on my own.

Taylor sure would make pretty babies. But we weren't even a couple for crying out loud.

I opened the shower door and turned on the water, keeping it cool to ease my growing heat. I haven't forgotten our chemistry. It was electric and not easy to ignore.

I stepped under the chilly water and let out a sigh. Turning my face up to the stream did little to temper the heat racing through my blood.

I quickly scrubbed my body and washed my hair. I dried off, wound my hair up, applied a bit of eye shadow, liner, and mascara. I touched my lips with tinted gloss. Still a bit damp, I struggled into a pair of jean shorts and pulled on a white tank top. I slung a belt around my hips and decided I looked fine in the Cheval mirror. Grabbing my bag, I left the room, and Taylor met me at the bottom of the stairs.

"You look great," he said, and I smiled.

He held the front door open, and we walked onto the porch.

"Thanks." Those three simple words touched me deeply. He followed me around the side of his truck and opened the door for me.

"I figured we'd take mine, since yours is a bit big and difficult to find parking for."

I stepped up into his truck and looked at him. "That's very considerate of you."

Our eyes clung to each other for a few moments. I almost swayed toward him but caught myself. A smile crept up on the side of his mouth. He closed the door, and I watched him walk around the front of the truck. My heart beat a little harder, and it was difficult to breathe.

He climbed in beside me. The wide console was between us. I watched his smooth movements, the corded muscles in his forearms and the way the sleeve of his shirt stretched around his biceps and was tight over his powerful chest.

He certainly wasn't any kind of doctor I'd had growing up. My mouth was suddenly dry, and I dug in my bag for a mint. I held the package out to him.

"Mint?"

Taylor reached over and took one, and our fingers brushed. I sucked in a soft breath. Yup, we still had it.

On the heels of the rush of desire at the slight touch of

our fingers was a wonderful feeling of contentment. Belonging.

I settled comfortably in Taylor's truck as we drove through town. My original plan of exploring Oak Creek and then doing a bit of shopping had long since vanished. It sounded all so unnecessary compared to being beside him, riding high in his big truck.

It was splashy and quite obviously top of the line, fire-engine red with dove-gray leather seats. I sighed and relaxed rolling my head on the headrest to look at him. He was concentrating on the road, and I let my eyes rove over him.

I couldn't seem to get enough of looking at him today. His aviator glasses concealed his ice-blue eyes. He had a great profile. His nose had a little bump in it, and his lips were full and totally kissable. I should know.

When he smiled, the tiny gap between his otherwise even and white front teeth only enhanced his appearance. His hair had more salt and pepper than it did in Denver, and he kept it much shorter. I liked his look. It was unique and devilishly handsome in a wildly compelling way. He moved me to the core.

That's what attracted me to him in Denver. His allure definitely hadn't faded over the years since we'd been together. I tightened my thighs. My blood was still hot from the sexy vibes that came off him in waves.

Quiet and stealthy, I allowed myself to relive our sexual adventures as we drove through the streets of Oak Creek. Did I want to reignite what we'd had?

Goddamn right I did!

* * *

Taylor drove with no real destination in mind. He thought of a few places, but nothing turned his crank. He'd gotten to know Oak Creek more as the months went by since he moved here, but he still thought of himself as relatively new to town. He wanted to show Drea some of the places he'd discovered, but the list wasn't too long.

They were quiet as they drove. He was fine with it, and obviously, she was as well. It was nice they could be content in silence. With the windows open, the breeze blew in, and the smell of her soap and shampoo swirled around him. It was an exotic scent, making him think of sand, sun, palms, and them making love.

Okay, those kinds of thoughts will make it difficult to get through this nice day without any physical detours. She was looking out the window, and the wind drew her damp hair out of its bun so that tendrils fluttered around the frame of her face. He was breathless at her beauty.

He still recalled how soft her hair was, the smoothness of her skin, the way her legs wrapped around him. He was getting hard and tried to think of something else.

But there was no point. He'd had her in his arms not so long ago, and it had resulted in a renewed awakening for her. If things continued along this vein, and she felt the same, even though right now they were friends with no benefits, it would be impossible to resist each other.

They'd only shared a few moments here and there over the past weeks. Their work schedule kept them both busy.

Today was a refreshing change. Being able to go out together as normal people – not necessarily as a couple— was nice. He hadn't thought much about a relationship with anybody for quite some time. He'd put all of his energy into his career change and being at the top of his game.

But, there was something missing, and it had taken her living with him to recognize it.

He pulled up to a red light. They looked at each other before he glanced back at the lights, waiting for it to change to green. She was humming along to a tune on the radio.

Taylor liked having someone else in the house. It was nice and a complete surprise to him. When he was in his room trying to sleep, he liked hearing her in the house or her shower running. He enjoyed the sounds of her skipping up and down the stairs and talking to Cinder.

He didn't sleep much, maybe a few hours at a time. He spent the rest of his time reading or relaxing in his room, hoping sleep would take him. He couldn't remember the last time he'd slept through the night. So he was usually awake and listening to her moving quietly around the house. He knew she tried to be quiet, but he could hear a pin drop.

There was an awareness that he hadn't experienced before, and when the door clicked shut behind her, he waited to hear her vehicle turn on and the sound of it leaving the driveway before he was able to close his eyes and try to sleep.

Her hours were more awkward than his, and they came in at different times of the day, which was what they had anticipated when they originally decided to try cohabitation.

Once Drea left the house, Cinder searched him out. He'd lie on Taylor, finding a position on his chest whether he was sitting on the couch, lying in bed, or on a chair. He took up position with his butt close to Taylor's face and watched for Drea to come home. Taylor liked the cat, even if he was second fiddle. Which was another surprise.

"Do you fancy driving by the café to get another coffee?" she asked.

"Sure. It's just around the corner."

"Yes, I remember. I'm starting to get the lay of the land."

Taylor glanced at her, and she was smiling. She also held out a ten-dollar bill.

"You don't have to get it," he said.

She nodded. "Oh yes, I do. No freeloading. I have to pay my way, even if it's with coffee like this, or going out for groceries, contributing to a monthly bill."

The intensity on her face told him that she would not take no for an answer, and he respected that.

He took the bill from her as he pulled into the drive-through line. "Okay then. Later, we can look at the monthly bills. But I do want you to know that you don't have to help out financially at all. I wasn't expecting you to."

"I understand that, but you're helping me out in a time of need, especially with extra baggage. I really do want to pitch in."

"That's what friends are for." He pulled forward to place their order. "What do you want?"

"A grande caramel macchiato please."

"With whipped cream?"

"Of course, I forgot to mention it." She laughed, and he liked the sound of it filling his truck. He shook his head and smiled after giving their order through the speaker.

They drove up to the window and exchanged the money for the macchiato and his Americano.

"So where is the first stop?" Andrea asked him and then took a sip of her drink.

"I thought maybe we would just go that a-way." He pointed his finger out the windshield.

Drea laughed again, and he was heartened she seemed less wound up and tense. She was much more relaxed.

"Sounds good to me. I am at your mercy."

Taylor glanced at her and waggled his eyebrows. "Is that so?"

A blush stained her cheeks, charming him. He'd been teasing her and was pretty sure she realized what her words could imply.

"We can drive around Oak Creek. Or we can go further afield. There's a nice eatery out of town we could give a try. I've heard positive reviews. Or we could just stop along the way somewhere."

"I kinda like that idea. Yes, let's just drive." She pointed out the windshield as he had done.

"Your wish is my command."

They fell silent, and she reached over to turn the radio up. Finding some classic rock music, she sat back and appeared to be enjoying the drive. A song came on, and she began to sing. It was a Nora Jones song that he hadn't heard before. It was all about turning her on.

Drea had a lovely voice, and he enjoyed listening to her soft words matching with the artist's. When the song was over, another one came on, and she also sang along to that one.

"You have a nice voice," he told her.

"Oh, don't be silly. I sound like I'm cackling. But whatever. I like to sing to songs that I know."

Do you do karaoke?" he asked

"Oh God, no. I'm a car singer only."

"Well, that's interesting. Why wouldn't you sing karaoke if you sing in the car? I bet you're good enough to win a contest."

"Oh no, no, no. I can't sing in front of a crowd. The very

thought of it gives me the chills. You know that movie My Best Friend's Wedding? The karaoke part at the dinner? And how bad Cameron Diaz's voice was? That would be me. Yup, me at a karaoke bar."

Taylor laughed. He knew that scene.

"Okay then, sing away. Maybe I'll even sing along with you." That was something he hadn't done for years.

"Deal."

They continued to drive. The scenery was gorgeous, and she looked out the window as she belted out some of the songs.

"Time Warp" came on, and she let out a shout that startled him. "You have to know this one."

"Do I now? What if I don't?"

"Just shut up and sing," she ordered him.

He laughed and joined in, singing and realized he was having fun. She danced in her seat, doing all the right moves in time to the music.

She tilted her head and made a comical face while she sang about slipping to the right and jumping to the left with hands on your hips while wiggling in the seat.

Taylor cracked up, and her smile widened while she continued singing "Time Warp". She was so full of life.

They hadn't gotten to know each other too much on their weekend, but they were now, and he liked everything he was learning about her.

Something was changing in him. He felt the shift, and Taylor decided not to fight it, not to overthink and to simply enjoy the day.

What will be, will be.

Did I really just tell myself that? Taylor shook his head. Yep, things were definitely changing.

Chapter Fourteen

I was having the best time. This impromptu road trip was exactly what I needed. I could literally feel myself relaxing and melting into the truck seat. It was wonderful.

This trip put our relationship into a different category. We weren't just roommates now. We were friends.

And yes, I did secretly hope for more. Everything had been a whirlwind since I arrived. I was glad we knew each other from before, because it was helping me to settle in.

We were easy together. Which I hadn't expected with our very hot sexual history, and now we were getting to know each other. We were doing it kind of backward.

He was fun, and his sense of humor was starting to reveal itself. He had seemed broody and intense when I first arrived in Oak Creek, and the more time I spent with him, the more I realized there was a quietness about him. As if something heavy weighed him down. But then who was I to judge? I had my own baggage I was dragging around with me.

A sign on the road intrigued me. It was shaped like a

sunflower and had words in each petal. We got closer, and I could see the names of food trucks were printed on the petals and in the center were the words Sunflower Fields.

"Taylor, can we stop there?" I pointed to the sign as we approached.

"Lunch that includes wine tasting. Sounds like a plan to me."

"I am starting to get hungry. Your breakfast was good, but it didn't stick to the ribs," I teased him and enjoyed his laughter.

"Your wish is my command."

"I better come up with some better wishes to command you with." I grinned at him and was happy at his return smile. We approached another sign that told us to turn left, and we did. The road wound under a canopy of trees.

"No, this doesn't look sketchy at all, does it?" I said, thinking that maybe this was not the best idea.

"Where is your sense of adventure? If we like what we see, we can stay. If not, we can leave."

I nodded and rested my elbow on the window ledge. We emerged from the trees, and the sun hit us in a radiant golden light. I gasped as my eyes adjusted.

"Oh, would you look at this." Sunflowers fanned out into the fields in every direction.

"Well, well. Sometimes taking the road less traveled turns out to be a nice surprise." Taylor drove the truck into a parking lot also ringed by trees with parking spaces to keep cars cool under the branches.

I grabbed my wallet and stuck a sun hat on my head. I jumped out of the vehicle and waited for Taylor to come around to my side.

He took my hand, and I clasped his fingers. A surge of delight warmed me, and I couldn't bite back a happy smile.

We walked toward the little buildings. Almost like a town square. A vineyard fanned out in neat rows like spokes on a wheel opposite to the sunflower fields. We stopped in the center of the hub where tables sat under the arching tree branches and some people were seated.

The circle of food trucks ringed the central hub, and good summer music played on hidden speakers.

"What is this place? It's magical, and my mouth is watering. The aroma of the food is delicious." I leaned closer to Taylor. "You never heard of this place before?"

We walked down one of the paths toward a bright yellow and purple truck.

"I had no idea this was here. I don't often come this way, so unless there was word-of-mouth or some advertising, I never would have heard about it."

"Then we're lucky." He squeezed my hand in agreement, and it hit me we were walking around holding hands as if we were a couple. My toe caught on a stone, and he steadied me.

"Okay?" He looked down at me, and I nodded.

"All good. Just a little shocked by this." I held up our hands, and he looked at our intertwined fingers.

"Ha. I hadn't even realized we were holding hands." He looked at me as if to ask for permission, and I didn't let go of his fingers.

I rather liked holding hands with him. "Well then, I guess this is part of the whole what-will-be-will-be scenario." His elbow gently nudged my arm.

"I think you must be right." I smiled and decided to enjoy the moment and rested my head on his shoulder.

* * *

Taylor stood quietly, not wanting her to lift her head. He liked how she felt so close to him.

"What do you think you're going to get?" he asked.

"I don't know. Sometimes when there are too many choices, it makes deciding more difficult."

Drea looked around, and Taylor crossed his arms. They both spun slowly, taking in all the different, brightly painted trucks.

There were at least a dozen trucks offering food from around the world. He wasn't quite sure what he wanted.

"You know, maybe I'll get something completely different. Something from the farthest-away country."

"That's a great idea. What you think?"

"I like Thai, but I've had it a lot. So..." he continued to contemplate.

"You know what? I'm going to go for Polish sausage and pierogis," Drea said with determination.

"Ha. I hadn't even thought about that. But you know what, it sounds perfect."

He took her hand again and liked how it felt in his. Her head only came to his shoulders, and the overpowering urge to be protective was a new feeling for him.

Taylor glanced down at her and met her gaze. He smiled and squeezed her hand. He was rewarded with a grin and she tightened her hand in his. This road trip was turning out to be a great idea. It gave them the perfect opportunity to be together without any outside intrusion.

At the truck, they stood under the white and red canopy and looked at the menu.

"Holy cow, I didn't realize there would be so many options to choose from. All those toppings on a Polish sausage on a bun? I would've just put mustard on it," she said.

"It smells great. I think I'll get the one that has onions and cabbage and tomatoes." Taylor nodded, decision made.

"Oh look, they have Polish sausage cabbage rolls. On a bun. I'm totally getting that." He liked the excitement in her voice.

They stepped forward and placed their orders along with a large order of pierogis. He saw they also had pickled herring and sour cream and added it to their order.

Laden with a bag of lunch, they found a table under a tree. It was warm, but there were clouds scattered through the sky, and it was starting to get darker.

"Looks like a storm is closing in on us." Taylor sat and unpacked the bag of food.

"I heard we were going to be getting storms this afternoon, but it's coming in quicker than forecasted," she said while picking up her bun and looking for the best place to take the first bite.

"Hopefully, it doesn't rain until we finish lunch and get a chance to do some wine tasting." He took a bite of his roll, and flavor exploded in his mouth. "Mmm." He nodded.

"Right." Drea picked up a pierogi and swept it through the sour cream. "Oh, man."

"How did you find your way to Oak Creek?" he asked her.

"I tend to move around a lot, kind of go where the need takes me." She took a sip of her Dr. Pepper. "It was actually Shannon that told me about the opening, and that's how I found myself here."

She took another bite of her sandwich, and he dipped a piece of herring in the sour cream and also loaded some onion on it.

"I've never had herring." She grimaced.

"Have a try." Taylor pushed the plate toward her.

"I don't know."

"Come on. Be a taster. That's what my aunt would say when I was a kid and didn't want to eat something. Once you taste it, you can decide not to like it."

"If you insist." Drea picked a small piece and put it in her mouth.

Taylor watched her chew slowly. The bridge of her nose wrinkled, and she blinked a few times.

"Okay, I tasted." She took a quick drink.

"And?"

"Not awful, but not great. I think I'm just an English fish-and-chip kinda girl. How did you end up here, and why the change in career path?"

His tilted his head back and picked up the napkin to wipe his fingers. This time, it was Taylor who took a long drink while he considered his answer. He knew this question would come up eventually, and he still wasn't sure if he was ready to talk about it.

"I was offered the head of ER at Oak Creek Gen, which I couldn't pass up. The change in career path..." He shrugged and looked off over the fields. "Stuff happened, and I decided it would be best to make a change."

She was silent, but her eyes bored into him with an intensity that made him feel as if it was okay to spill his guts to her. He still wasn't able to move his lips to form words.

"It's okay, I get it. You don't want to talk about it." She picked up her sandwich and took a bite. "When you're ready to talk, I'm here."

He sensed a shift between them. They were slowly opening up and getting to know each other, but they still had a long way to go. He wanted to know her, and she wanted to know him. The only way to do that was by talking and sharing.

"Thanks, I appreciate it. It's not something I talk about much." He drew in a breath and let it out slowly. "It's something I felt responsible for, and it caused tremendous heartache. People died, and I was to blame."

He looked into her eyes and saw compassion.

"Could you have done anything differently?" she asked.

Taylor thought about it and nodded slowly. "Maybe, who knows really. Now, how about we finish up here and do that wine tasting. The sky looks like it's getting a little heavy."

* * *

We looked at the wine list.

"Shall we get a flight? Or just sample tasting?" I asked.

"How about we get a flight? You can drink most of it, and I'll taste some since I'm driving."

"I'll get smashed. But I'll have you to take care of me, right?" That thought warmed me. Wouldn't it be nice to be able to rely on someone instead of always being the responsible one? Maybe one day.

"Of course I will."

"I did want to do some shopping too."

"Why'd don't we play it by ear? At least you have a designated driver." He smiled, and his blue eyes crinkled nicely under his heavy brows. The sun peeked out between a dark cloud and sparkled off his hair.

He was a damn good-looking guy, and I swear I was getting more and more smitten. The little sprinkling of silver around the edges of his close-cropped hair enhanced his attractiveness. He was definitely going to be a silver fox. At least, I thought so anyway.

"Okay, sounds like a plan."

A short while later, a wooden board with very nice wine glasses was placed before us.

"Those glasses are gorgeous." They weren't too tall and had a unique sunflower design twisted up from the stem.

"They are. I bet we could buy a pair in the gift shop. All right, I'll take the first sip, and you take the gulp." Taylor chuckled.

"Funny guy. Shall we start at one end and work our way across?" I picked up the glass on the far right. It was a pale white wine. I handed him the glass. He took a sip and wrinkled his nose.

"Too sweet and fizzy."

I took the glass from him, swallowed a mouthful, and looked up at the sky, concentrating on the flavors in my mouth.

"Not bad. But I see what you mean." I put the glass back down on the board. "Number two." The next one was a little more golden but not sparkling. It was a Pinot Grigio with fermented fruit. I think the menu said apricots.

Taylor tried it. Bobbed his head side to side. "Not bad. A little fruity for my taste."

I took the glass and sniffed the liquid. "You like this one at all?" I asked him and took a drink of the Pino. This time, it was me that wrinkled my nose. "Nope. That makes me want to puke."

He burst out laughing, and some people at the table across from us looked our way to see what was so funny.

"And, yes, I do like this one. I'm more of a red-wine drinker than white, but we still have more on the board."

I put the glass down and reached for the next one, it was a Rosé Taylor took it from me, our fingers touched, and the familiar electric charge sizzled between us. We both paused for a beat, and I thought how nice the afternoon was going.

He took the glass, drank, and nodded. "Yep, I like that. It's fresh and flavorful without biting back."

I extended my hand and wiggled my fingers. "Give me." I smiled at him.

I tipped the glass, watching the wine swirl around. It had nice legs, and the aroma was divine.

I took a drink, and the flavor burst in my mouth. It was wonderful. I took a second sip and savored the velvety luxuriousness in my mouth.

"Do you like that one?" Taylor said and reached for the next one on the board. "You finish it," he said when I held the glass to him.

"Yes, I do. We'll have to get some to take home." I finished the wine and loved the sensation of it going down my throat and the way it warmed my belly. Then I realized I'd said home. Whether it was the wine or referring to Taylor's house as home, I didn't know, but a contentment filled me. I watched Taylor through my now sorta tipsy eyes.

"We sure can, maybe a box."

"A box? You'd really buy a box of wine." My words slurred slightly, and I clamped my mouth shut. I'd always been a cheap drunk.

He nodded and handed me a glass of the red. "Of course. If you like it, we'll get a box and store it in the cellar."

I sipped the red wine. I did like reds, but I had to be careful. If the tannins were too high, I could tell immediately and would get heartburn. This one had a barnyard aroma, it added a layer of complexity to the wine, which could be good, but I wasn't normally a fan. I took a mouthful. It was smooth but when I swallowed, I could feel the burn in my esophagus.

I shook my head." "No, I don't want to finish this. I know it will give me heartburn. Feel free."

He took the goblet from me, and again, our fingers brushed. The sensation of his skin on mine coupled with the buzz I was getting from the drinks was the perfect recipe for smexy times. I didn't even bother to try and ignore the sexual desire building.

I mean, how could I not feel this? I was highly attracted to Taylor. I knew how we were together. The wine gave me a little more confidence, and his presence was all just too much for me to deny.

I wanted him.

We were silent and stared into each other's eyes. I ached to lean over the table and kiss him. To have his hands on me. The slow and sensual smile curving his lips told me he felt it too.

Taylor picked up the last glass and held it up to look at the color against the sky.

"This, I have a feeling, will be more my style." He swirled the glass like I had and smiled.

When he had some in his mouth, he closed his eyes and tilted his head back as if he'd just died and gone to heaven.

"Good?" I asked him.

He nodded slowly and opened his eyes, pinning me with his. God help me, he looked so good it made my belly flip over.

He was handing the glass to me and stopped midway. He furrowed his eyebrows. "What's that look for?"

I shook myself out of my daydream. "Oh, what look? I was just thinking about how much you must like that wine." *Actually, I want to jump into bed with you.*

A slow smile spread across his lips, and something told me he knew that's not what I was thinking about. Strangely,

I didn't really mind that he may suspect my carnal thoughts. Living with him is extremely tempting and so far we'd been very good. How easy it would be to go down the hall in the dark of night and climb into bed with him? Was he thinking the same thing as me?

I hope so.

Taylor handed me the last glass and I slowly lifted it to my mouth not taking my eyes off him. He watched my mouth. The wine was delicious, and I swallowed, enjoying the bright flavors.

Now I knew I couldn't stem the desire growing inside me. It was overpowering, and I was barely able to breathe. If we kept at it much longer, we wouldn't get farther than his truck before–

Again, I shook myself out of my daydream. "Ah, yup, I like this one."

"Where were you a moment ago, Drea?" he asked with a crooked smile.

"Uhm, where was I? I-I nowhere. Here." I fibbed the little white lie. "Here drinking wine with you in the middle of a vineyard and food-truck place."

He reached his hand across the table and laid it over mine. That was my undoing. Liquid heat fired through me, and my nipples pushed against my top. I had to cross my legs from the throbbing heat that flared between them.

"I think I know what you're dreaming about. Because I am too." His voice held that low, gravelly I want to get you into bed tone I heard so often in Denver.

Air whooshed out of me, and I turned my hand over so I was holding his.

"Really? This is all so complicated. Isn't it?"

He tilted his head to the side. "Complicated? It doesn't have to be. I don't see complications."

I thought about it and wondered how he could not see the complications. Our agreement in Denver, my tendency to pick up and leave and find a new place to live. Whatever it was that caused him to switch careers.

I pulled my hand out from him, missing his touch even if it had been very brief.

* * *

It was dark when Taylor pulled into his driveway. He glanced over at Drea. She was fast asleep with her head resting back against the headrest and the side of the truck. She was snoring gently, and her face was relaxed. He didn't think he'd seen her face so relieved of stress and worry since she'd arrived. He turned off the truck. He got out and unlocked the house so he could carry her in. At the truck, he maneuvered her into his arms, and was surprised she didn't wake up.

He smiled. It was probably the wine combined with sheer exhaustion. He cradled her and liked it when she reached up and pressed her hand to his chest and turned her face into him. It was an unconscious move, but it told him a lot. She knew he was there and she was safe. His chest swelled and almost ached with a raw and unexpected emotion coupled with desire and the need to take care of her. Protect her.

Drea continued to sleep when he went in the front door, closed it, and climbed the stairs. He carried her into her bedroom.

Her bed was neatly made, so he laid her on top, took the quilt draped over the iron footboard, and gently placed it over her.

She murmured in her sleep and rolled to her side. Her

hand fell over the edge of the bed. Taylor tucked it under the quilt. Before he could let go, she curled her fingers around his.

She moaned and her eyes fluttered. "Stay."

Taylor's chest almost exploded. How he wanted to stay with her. There was no question, and he hesitated for a moment, deciding what to do.

She tugged his hand. "Stay... Hold me."

He couldn't refuse her and lay on the bed behind her. She snuggled into his chest, her back curved into his front. He put his arm under her pillow and hugged her close

She sighed, and he was so moved that his throat tightened. "I've got you," he whispered into her hair.

Soon, she was breathing deeply, and he knew she was asleep. He did his best to remain still, so he didn't disturb her. He wanted this magical moment to last.

He had her in his arms. He vowed the trust she'd placed in him would never be misplaced. He would be there regardless. In the morning, they would talk about their plans. Their future.

Taylor was aroused, but he pushed it down. Now definitely wasn't the time. He wanted her awake, ready and eager for when they decided to make love. He felt it was important for them to dive deeper and get to know each other much better. He wanted to know what made her tick, what made her happy or sad. He pressed a kiss to her head, liking how her hair fanned over the pillow.

There was so much he wanted to discover about her.

He didn't expect to sleep. He rarely slept. Slowly, his eyes drifted closed, and he tightened his hold on Drea, never wanting to let her go.

* * *

A feather was tickling my nose. When I reached up to scratch, I felt my hand brush across soft, curling hair. Sometimes I had lucid dreams where I knew where I was even though I was still dreaming, and this must be one of them. If it wasn't a feather and it was hair, was I dreaming or was I awake? I pressed my hand into the softness and came against warm muscled flesh.

A man's chest. I snuggled in closer, liking this dream. I hadn't had a man for so long, and the one in this dream was perfect. A muscled arm draped over my shoulders, and I curled my arms into my chest, letting myself be pulled against him. I was wrapped in safety, warm and protected.

I sighed deeply, the man of my dream was almost real. I pressed my cheek against his chest, inhaled his wonderful scent and drifted off.

This was rather peculiar, because I was dreaming I was falling asleep again. It was too complicated to try and figure it out, so I let it slide out of my mind and into the weightlessness of oblivion.

A sound woke me, and I listened with my eyes still closed. It was purring and soft snores from somebody beside me. I opened my eyes. In the dim light of dawn, I saw the outline of Cinder curled up on Taylor's chest. He was fast asleep beside me. I remained still, not wanting to wake either of them.

I lay there trying to remember what had happened yesterday. I was still dressed, but Taylor was bare chested, and we both lay on top of the covers.

My sleepy brain recalled our lunch at the vineyard and the wine flight, but the rest of the day faded into nothingness. I didn't think I was drunk, but maybe the wine relaxed me into a sound sleep.

I didn't even remember the drive home or getting into

bed. I sat up a little more to watch the two males next to me sleeping. Cinder opened his eyes, and I looked at me. I reached over to stroke his ears. He tipped his head and placed his nose on Taylor's chest.

Aww.

I watched Taylor sleep. I wasn't alarmed we were in bed together. After all, we'd been here and done that before. I watched them both for a little while until my eyelids grew heavy again. I rolled onto my side, pushing the pillow under me, and I laid my hand on Taylor's belly. The tip of Cinder's tail gently waved back and forth.

The next thing I knew, an alarm beeped. I was awake in an instant, thinking it was a smoke detector going off. I sniffed and didn't smell anything. Taylor was still sleeping beside me, and Cinder was curled up between us. Taylor's eyes moved behind his lids, and he yawned.

"Hey there," I said softly.

He looked at me in confusion. "Oh hey. There's sleeping beauty. What time is it anyways?"

I looked at the time on my phone. "Eight thirty."

He stretched and sat up against the iron bed frame propping the pillows behind him. Cinder expressed his disapproval that we'd disturbed his slumber and jumped off the bed, thumping to the wooden floor, with a disgruntled meow.

"We must've slept right through the night," I said as I swung my legs over the edge of the bed and sat for minute, curling my toes.

"Must've. I haven't slept like that in years."

I looked over my shoulder at him. "What do you mean?"

He shrugged his shoulders, which were beautifully tattooed. I didn't remember the tattoos from before.

"These are new." I traced my fingers over the intricate ink.

"I got them a few years ago. Sort of a therapy thing."

"I like them."

"I'm glad you do." He smiled and continued. "Basically, I don't sleep. I get a couple hours a night, and maybe some in the day. But sleep evades me as a rule. We must've slept at least ten hours. It's unheard of for me."

I leaned over and kissed him, murmuring against his lips. "I guess it must be me."

"Must be."

He caught me in his arms, and I didn't resist.

Chapter Fifteen

"Yeah, we did sleep." But, did we do anything else?

"Last night, ah, did—

"Anything happen?" he answered for me.

I looked into his eyes. Honesty, caring, and peace reflected back at me.

"Yes, I guess that's what I'm asking," I whispered. Not sure if I wanted something to happen or not. I was leaning to not because I wanted to be fully aware, and it would've been wrong on his part to take advantage. I trusted him, and that was a big deal.

He smiled and cupped the back of my head. "No. You don't need to worry. You were asleep." He smiled, and I couldn't help but giggle a little, which was uncharacteristic of me. For crying out loud. "I would never do anything like that. Taking advantage of unconscious women is not on my repertoire."

I nodded, relieved. "That's a good thing. I want to remember it, not have to be told about it." I smiled and lost myself in his gaze.

He gave me a gentle tug, and I let myself fall over his

chest, his other hand brushed the hair off my face. I gave a gentle shiver of delight.

"But we can change that now, if you like?" He cradled the back of my head, and I continued to gaze into his blue eyes.

I had no words to answer. Instead, I nodded, and he pulled me into his arms and rested his forehead against mine. "I never thought I'd see you again," he said in a low, gravelly voice.

"Me either. But that's what we agreed on at the time," I whispered.

He nodded. "Yes, we did. But I couldn't forget you."

I rested back into the crook of his arm, enjoying the warmth that flowed through my veins, and the way he gazed at me made my heart beat quicker.

Being next to him again after all these years was surreal.

"Neither could I." I reached my hand and ran my fingers over his short-cropped hair, loving the velvety feel. I pulled him toward me until our lips met, and like at the top of the stairs, it was electric.

We definitely still had chemistry. Being here with him was all I wanted right now. He pulled me on top of him, and I straddled his hips. I moaned, feeling the strength of his arousal between my legs. Our lips clung together and his hand roamed under my tank top, pushing it up and then over my head. He unsnapped my bra without any hesitation, and removed it. My head fell back, and I closed my eyes, loving the touch of his hands on my sides and breasts.

"Oh, Taylor," I breathed his name.

"You're just as gorgeous as I remember," Taylor said as he sat up to nuzzle his face between my breasts. He kissed my skin until he found a hard peak and pulled it gently between his lips. I held his head close to me as he lapped and sucked, driving me crazy with desire. I'd heard you could have an orgasm from nipple stimulation, but I've never believed it until now.

Taylor curled his arms around Drea's shoulders and pulled her in tightly. He'd hoped they would come to this place together, both of them agreeing to be together and reigniting the passion they'd shared.

He wasn't sure how quickly it would happen, and it was important for him that Drea initiated. But he hadn't expected it so soon. He wasn't complaining, not in the least, having been with her before only made him crave her more.

He realized now how important their weekend in Denver was to him. Now that she was here with him, he entertained the idea they could possibly make a future together. He realized it wasn't something that would happen overnight. It would take time.

He buried himself deep within her, giving her the pleasure she deserved. He'd remapped every inch of her body, loving the way she responded to him, and they both held each other as their climax enveloped them. She gasped and made a cry of pleasure before she flopped over him. It couldn't be more perfect. Her heart beat against his chest, and their breathing matched in time.

They lay quietly, and the sheen of exertion on their skin slowly evaporated. He rubbed his palm over her shoulder and down her arm to her hip and her arm draped over his waist.

"Wow." Drea's breath fluttered against his neck where she'd buried her face.

"Okay?" he asked her.

Drea rolled onto her side so she could look at him.

She nodded and smiled. "Mmm, very."

"I'm glad. No regrets?"

She shook her head and placed her palm on his cheek. Her hand was warm and soft. He turned his face to kiss her skin. She shook her head. "I'm glad."

After a few minutes laying quietly in each other's arms, Taylor said. "I'm going to have a shower. Care to join me?" He gave her a crooked grin.

"As long as it is just a shower. Don't get any ideas now." She rolled away and bounded out of the bed. He watched her dash into the bathroom, enjoying the view of her naked back and heart-shaped behind. The water turned on, and he jumped out of bed after her.

Taylor couldn't believe how great he felt. He'd had an amazing sleep and experienced wonderful intimacy making love to Drea. He couldn't remember the last time he'd felt so happy.

The scent of pineapple drifted on the steam out of the bathroom. Taylor smiled, liking the feminine scents that had begun to overtake his house.

From the doorway, he saw her from behind the glass wall of the shower. He closed the bathroom door to let steam fill the room. He remembered she liked her showers hot. She didn't hear him approach when he stepped inside.

Soaping his hands, he slid them across her back and shoulders. She didn't say anything, and when he massaged her neck, and dropped her head forward.

He continued to run his hands over the warm slipperiness of her skin, working down her shoulders and arms and back up under her sides to encircle and cup her breasts. His erection grew, and she pushed her butt back into him, arching herself against his chest.

Her breasts were wonderfully firm, and her nipples rose

up under his thumbs. She reached behind them to grasp his hips. Her nails dug into his ass cheeks, but the pain was necessary to bank his arousal a little bit. He wanted to bring her closer to the edge. To tease her.

With one hand, he cradled her breasts on his forearm, and with the other, he slowly slid down her taut belly to her folds where he found her nub that he could work magic on before slipping lower to find her center with his fingertips. She sagged in his arms.

Her head fell back on his shoulder as he sweetly tormented her until her body tensed with her orgasm. He pumped his hips, sliding his cock between the firm globes of her buttocks.

She whispered, "Come, Taylor. I want you to come on me."

Her words took him over the edge. He groaned into her neck with one last push as he did as she commanded and let himself come. He growled, unable to remain silent. He braced his legs, needing to keep them from sliding to the floor, and he held her tightly almost losing control of his muscles on the waves of his orgasm. He couldn't... never wanted, to let her go. Slowly he found his balanced again and drew in a ragged breath.

She turned, and they clung to each other, the hot water sluicing down them. He muttered, "fuck, that was incredible."

She reached between them, stroked his length, and cupped his balls.

His body jerked at her touch. "You gotta give me a minute. " he murmured against her mouth. "You're killing me."

She tipped her head and looked up at him. "Well, if I know you, that minute won't be very long."

Water streamed over her features, making her mouth look so wet, glossy, full, and very inviting. Taylor held her cheeks between his hands and lowered his head, gazing into her eyes. He crashed his mouth down on hers.

Her tongue was waiting for his. They met and played, and he groaned into her mouth. The way she arched her back and pressed her breasts to his chest, her nipples hard and insistent, undid him.

They kissed, and their hands explored each other under the rain of water until it chilled and forcing them out of the shower. Taylor wrapped a towel around her shoulders, and she handed him one. They dried each other off. There was no need to speak as they tended to each other with a gentleness that almost choked him up.

Drea gazed up at him. "You know what? I think I've worked up a bit of a hunger." She pushed her damp hair back off her face.

He smiled. "We didn't eat much after yesterday's late lunch. Fancy some pancakes and bacon?"

"Kali's?"

"You must be reading my mind."

He liked how her eyes lit up. She was happy. In that instant, Taylor knew he wanted to continue to make her happy. Her smile and dancing eyes were like the sun coming out from a dark cloud. A dark cloud that had hovered over him for far too long.

* * *

Our server slid the breakfast plates in front of us. I looked down at the stack of pancakes, side of bacon, and hash browns and couldn't wait to dive in.

"I discovered this place the day after I arrived. One of

the firefighters from the fire scene interrupted my break-fast," I told Taylor as I spread butter nice and thick over my pancakes.

"What guy? Did he give you his name?" he asked and drowned his pancakes in syrup.

"No, he did look familiar, but I don't know from where, because I don't recall seeing him at the scene." I shrugged and took a forkful of pancake with a piece of bacon. "Mmm, so good. When Shannon and I had dinner the other night at the bar, he was there too, and she shooed him away. She said she knows who he is. Said he's a bit of an outsider but harmless."

"Good to know. It worries me though, with the threats you've had recently."

I paused with my coffee mug halfway to my mouth and looked at Taylor. He was cutting a piece of bacon, but his forehead was furrowed, eyebrows bunched up, and he was frowning. My heart swelled seeing the concern etched on his face.

"Taylor."

He looked up at me.

"Please don't worry. I'm sure it's just some whacko who doesn't intend any real harm. Thank you for your concern. You know, I can handle myself," I said gently.

"Oh, I'm pretty sure you can. But it's not a bad idea to have people watch your back now, is it?"

I nodded while he chewed and stabbed another pile of pancakes. "Yes, it is nice to know you have my back." Maybe I should change the subject. "Yesterday was nice."

His smile was enough to brighten anybody's day. "Yes, it was. I'm glad you enjoyed yourself."

"I really did."

He was gentlemanly enough to not bring up this morning. He was leaving that for me.

I swirled pancake and bacon through the syrup. "Thanks for washing my hair this morning." I grinned, and he laughed.

"Any time. I was happy to help." The sexual intensity in his expression made me gasp softly. All I wanted now was to whisk him outta here and have my way with him. I gripped my fork a little tighter and selected more food.

Our relationship had taken a bit of a turn. We'd gone from being only acquaintances with a spicy past to being lovers and possibly building a relationship. Not to mention working together as it warranted.

I wasn't really surprised by the shift into a physical relationship with him. I hadn't been able to put it out of my mind since we first stumbled across each other at the first fire scene.

We ate quietly for the next little while, comfortable in the quiet. To me, that showed we were used to each other and didn't feel the need to fill the silence with small talk.

I looked around. The restaurant was full, and a waiting line had started. I didn't recognize anyone. I suppose I still had a while until I felt totally at home in Oak Creek.

I thought about the guy I'd mentioned to Taylor earlier. I hadn't seen him since dinner with Shannon, and to be honest, I was glad. He gave me the creeps.

"What do you think about me talking to the fire chief about that guy?" I asked Taylor.

He glanced up. "The one that you saw here?"

"Yeah, there is something off, and I've been to a couple of fires since arriving here that were suspicious. Just old, abandoned barns where there was no reason for them to go up unless it was arson." I swirled a piece of bacon in a puddle of maple syrup and went over those fires in my mind.

"Maybe you should, especially if you think there is a connection to him and the fires." He paused with the fork almost at his mouth. "Trust your gut."

"That's just it. I don't know if there is a connection, but my gut is telling me something's up."

Yes, I could tell the fires were suspicious. No, there were no suspects. Yes, I was starting to suspect we had a serial arsonist. I'd made reports to the local police and the chiefs. Everyone was on alert and prepared. Once final reports came back on a few pieces of evidence, I'd have a better idea of the cause.

"Penny for your thoughts," Taylor said and put his napkin on his plate, sat back, and nursed a second cup of coffee.

"Just thinking about those barn fires."

"I don't think I heard about them," he said and lifted his mug.

"Hmm, there really isn't much to say. I think it's an arsonist, but we don't have any suspects. We're still waiting on evidence," I told him.

"Well, I'm sure he'll eventually make a mistake and fall into your lap."

"I hope so. But there's something about it that's really bugging me. You know, like when you can't quite remember something."

I reached for my mug and tilted it to see how much was left. A last gulp. "I should go through some of my case files and see if there are any similarities to the previous fires."

Taylor frowned. "How could there be similarities?"

"I meant cause, what started the fire. I'd also like to cross check fire causes in Oak Creek and some from my previous job as well." I gazed out the window and glanced up briefly when the waitress filled my mug. Just as I was turning to thank her, I saw a face out of the corner of my eye that made my blood run cold. I froze, afraid to turn and double-check.

"What?" Taylor leaned forward, and I swiveled my gaze to him.

My mouth was dry, and I gulped some coffee to unstick my tongue from the roof of my mouth. I slowly turned to look out the window, afraid of what I might see.

"What's wrong? What do you see? Drea, tell me." Taylor reached over and touched my hand, making me jump.

"Ah, I think I saw s-s-someone outside who reminds me of..."

I faced Taylor. I didn't want him to be concerned. I didn't want to be responsible for someone else worrying over me, so I played it down.

I knew what it was like to love and lose. But I had to remind myself I wasn't the only person in the world who had.

Alarm was etched on his features, and I knew since arriving in Oak Creek, my feelings for Taylor had grown. Last night and this morning proved it. We were more than fuck buddies from Denver.

He reached over and took my hand. "Okay, whoever you saw, they're gone now." He gazed in the direction I had been looking, and of course, there was no one in sight. "Okay now?"

I met Taylor's eyes. I wanted to say no, it's not okay, but I couldn't bring myself to. If I did that, I would drag Taylor into it, because I knew he wouldn't let it go.

The parking lot was full, just as it was inside the restaurant. I searched everyone's face to try and jog my memory and see if I was being watched. Nothing.

Drawing in a deep breath, I gave Taylor a tremulous smile. I didn't want him to worry.

I wasn't positive about who I just saw. It couldn't be him anyway, because he's in jail.

* * *

After we got home from our breakfast, I pulled out the banker box I'd brought. It held notes from some of my files. They weren't originals. Those stayed with my previous employer. These were my personal notations for some of the bigger cases as well as copies of some images that would be a valuable reference for future investigations.

If I wanted more detail, I'd have to reach out to my old boss for access. For now, I'd stick with these, and if it became necessary, I'd send an email.

My departure had been on good terms, the fire investigators office had been grooming me for management. I was honored, but I wasn't ready for it because it meant I would have to put down roots, settle into one place and stay a while.

I wasn't good at that. I knew it stemmed back to the fire that took my childhood home, my father, and set me on the path I'm now on.

I respect fire, even if it terrifies me. I'd become an obsessive checker. I always made sure any potential fire hazards were dealt with and didn't allow smoking inside. Had I gotten better over the years? It was hard to say. Maybe.

I don't often think about that day. It scared me in a way that I continue to deal with today. A nine-year-old losing everything she knew in the blink of an eye was a profound way to begin life. Dad had died in the fire while trying to save us. He did, but the old farmhouse had gone up like a candlestick, and when he went back in to get whatever it was—we never did find out—the upstairs had crashed down on him.

We stood watching in horror as the fire seemed to be alive. The sounds coming from the house had given me nightmares, the way it moaned, and seemed to scream it's anger into the night sky. I imagined the flames were picking and choosing who and what it wanted to burn. As if it had a life of its own.

Mom had put her arms around us, held us tightly, and all I'd wanted to do was run up to the house and scream at the blaze. But she had me in a vise grip, and by the time fire department had finally arrived. It was too late to save Dad or the house.

After that I don't remember much. Mom had us in therapy to help, and maybe it did, maybe it didn't. How do we really know? I certainly knew I carried grief and trauma from that day.

What I do know is it led to a life of Mom, Christine, and I living on people's couches and depending on the generosity of friends and family. Until the insurance money came in, we were transient. It was a lifestyle that had followed me into adulthood.

I pushed the feelings down, smothered them by focusing on my work and the task at hand. I needed to find what I was searching for.

I pulled the notebooks out and stacked them on the table, glad I'd kept them. I didn't think I'd need them, but seeing—or at least thinking I'd seen—someone from my past had shaken me. I hated to admit it, even to myself. But it had.

The person I was thinking of was still in jail. He had to be. It wasn't possible for him to be out yet... I wracked my brain, trying to recall something that hung like a shadow in the corner of my mind. The case had been years ago. I sat back on the chair, holding the lid to the banker's box, and thrummed my fingers on it, frowning.

Think, think. What was it?

Puffing out a sigh, I dropped the lid beside the box on the bed. I reached in and walked my fingers over the tops of the file folders. They were labeled and filed alphabetically and then chronological. I kept an up-to-date printout on top of the folders with the case number, date, victim(s), structure I.D., suspect, and conclusion printed. If I had my computer, it would be searchable by all fields. I was a bit of a spreadsheet freak. But my computer was still en-route with my vehicle and other household items. They were ridiculously behind schedule.

So old school would have to do.

I pulled my lower lip between my teeth. What was I missing? While I ran my fingertips over the tops of the file folders, I went through the alphabet in my head.

A - B - C all the way to Z. A trick I did to help jog my memory. Sometimes it took a couple of run-throughs until I homed in on the evasive information.

This time, it took only a second before I fell on the letter B.

"Yep, it was him. But it couldn't be," I murmured and looked for my arson folder on Benjamin Clark. The person I saw reminded me of him. But he was incarcerated and would be for a while yet.

I shook my head, flipped open the folder, and ran my fingertip down the table of contents I had at the beginning of each file. He was a particularly nasty dude, and it had taken two and half years to nail him. He'd always been one step ahead of us. Like he had some kind of fire background, but he'd refused to discuss that in the trial or when being questioned.

Nowadays, all anyone had to do was go online and search whatever it was that they wanted, whether it be good or bad. Of course, online access has also made it easy for those with unsavory tendencies. They can find pretty much anything they wanted. All the step-by-step instructions right there accessible for all.

It was a shocking and nasty part of my job to see the end results of people that played with fire.

The file didn't shed any light for me. I refreshed my memory on the case, read the notes, and digested it. I definitely would be on alert from now on.

Hyper-vigilance and I were old friends. I'd grown up being highly aware of my surroundings. Sometimes going a bit overboard in regards to fire safety, and I was always aware of any fire hazards. It was an after-effect from the fire that destroyed my early years and childhood home.

While I was putting away the banker's box, my phone pinged. I was being called out to a fire.

Chapter Sixteen

When I got back from the call, I finally found the time to email my old boss for confirmation on Benjamin Clark. He replied that he was still incarcerated and there was no way he could be here.

While that was good to know because it meant he was still locked up, it also left open the who. Who had I seen? Who was writing these awful notes?

I'd finished up some reports and was eager to get home and chill. On the way to my truck, I saw paper fluttering on the windshield. I let out a sigh and tilted my head as I walked over. What the heck now?

I'd had it with these weird notes and damage to the vehicle. Enough was enough. I snatched the sheet from under the windshield wiper, holding the corner in case the police wanted to do any forensics on it.

Did I want to see what it said? Sometimes blissful ignorance can be good, but in this case, I needed to know. Right? For multiple reasons. One being my mind would run rampant and only cause more worry.

I had to know, which meant facing what was on the

note. First, I walked around and checked the vehicle. I circled the truck, giving all the tires a kick and looking for any new scratches or marks. So far so good.

I climbed into the driver seat and held the paper, staring at it. It looked normal enough, just a plain white sheet of paper.

I sighed, knowing that ignoring what was on the page was the coward's way out. As well as careless. Holding the corner between my thumb and forefinger, I gave the paper a little shake, and it fell open.

I gasped, and a chill ran down my spine. I wasn't expecting the gruesome image of a burned body, and it startled me. I had to force myself to breathe slowly so my heart would stop pounding.

Who would do such a thing?

I dropped the note on the seat beside me, but it fluttered to the floor. I didn't bother to pick it up and leaned back in the seat with my eyes closed. It hurt to breathe, and I tried to calm myself, or I'd have a heart attack or stroke or something. Why was I being targeted?

I fumbled for my phone, not finding it right away. Another moment of panic. Had I lost it? Did I leave it in the office? I briefly entertained the notion that whoever wrote the note had taken my phone.

I leaned over the console and shoved aside my bag. There it was. I let out a sigh of relief and grabbed it, opened the app and called Taylor on video chat. He answered right away.

"What's up?"

"I got another note." I heard the breathlessness of my voice and inhaled deeply.

His brows furrowed, and he pinned me with an intense gaze. God, I wished he was with me right now.

"Show me." His voice hard.

"Hang on. I dropped it, and it's on the floor." I leaned down to pick it up.

"Are the doors locked?"

"I-I don't... Ah, no they're not."

"Lock them."

I sat up and glanced around. "Now you're scaring me," I told him.

"If you're in your truck, you're fine. Just make sure you lock the doors. You don't know who this person is, and as long as you're alone, you're vulnerable."

I gritted my teeth, biting back the anger surging through me. One minute I was worried, even afraid, and the next minute I was madder than a wet cat.

"Fucking guy!" I shouted and hit the steering wheel.

"Show me the note." Taylor's voice was calm and firm.

I held it up in front of the camera so he could see it.

"Holy shit. I think you need to take that to the police. Where are you now?"

"I'm in the fire marshal's parking lot about to head home. I found this piece of crap on the windshield."

Taylor grinned.

"What's so funny? This isn't funny." I was about to explode from frustration.

"I'm not laughing at you, honest. Your anger is a new element to you." I didn't feel any better. He continued, "Okay. drive over to Oak Creek P.D. and show them this note. You are a government employee being threatened by someone. They need to be aware so they can deal with it."

I started the truck and turned on the air con. It had begun to get warm in the cab, and I was fuming, which made my temperature boil.

"Okay, I'm heading over there now."

"Good, I'll meet you. Now go," he instructed.

My heart raced on the drive over. By the time I pulled into the lot at the station, I had better control. The anger still simmered, but a new emotion began to take root. And I didn't like it.

For the first time, I was scared. All this shit was disquieting and was making me angry as well. The threats were getting worse and more sinister in nature. Before getting out of the truck, I looked around and checked my mirrors to make sure no one was lurking around my vehicle.

I put the paper in an empty file folder, got out, and all but ran into the station. Taylor was already waiting for me.

"What, did you fly here?"

"I was closer."

I fell into his arms, his presence giving me strength. I clung to him, holding back the tears of frustration. Damn, the last thing I wanted was to be this wilting violet. My body trembled, and I couldn't stop it.

"It's alright. Now let's go talk to the duty desk sergeant, yes?"

I nodded and quickly swiped the back of my hand over my cheeks. "Okay."

"Right, come on. Do you want to do the talking or me?"

I looked up at him. "I can do it. It just means a lot that you're here with me now. This is getting way too much." After checking in with the duty desk, we sat in the chairs to wait. About ten minutes later, an officer called us in.

"Hey, Tay. Surprised to see you here."

"Yeah, I'm here for moral support. Drea is here to see you."

The officer pulled out a chair for me and Taylor and shifted his belt so he could also sit.

"So, Drea, tell me what this is about?"

I put the folder on the table, flipped it open, and turned it around so he could see.

He leaned over, and with the tip of his pen, pulled the folder toward him.

"Okay," he said. "Can you give me some context around this?"

He didn't look alarmed or worried, just like it was an everyday occurrence for someone to come into the station and show him such a gruesome image.

My anger spiked. Not at him, but it certainly did come across that way.

"This is a new one, I just got it today. There have been others." My voice shook, and my words were rushed. Taylor's hand settled on my thigh, calming me. I drew in a shaky breath.

The officer didn't look offended at my tone. He just quietly watched me. I needed to get it together. I was a professional, after all, and this sort of thing should be much easier to handle.

"Sorry. I'm pissed off, and I hate to admit I'm scared too. This isn't the first time either. I filed a report on vehicle damage a couple of weeks ago."

"Do you have the occurrence number?"

"I do." I opened my bag, took the slip of paper out of my wallet, and gave him the number. He pulled it up on the computer. He was nodding his head and read the file.

"Ah, okay. You're the new fire marshal. I see your other report here. This does seem to be a bit of an escalation."

"Yes, I thought so," I said, agreeing with him.

"Right, I want you to write down what happened." He pushed a pad of paper and pen over to me. While I started to make notes, he continued, "You have no idea who could be doing this?" he asked.

I glanced at him and shook my head. "No. I just moved here for this job a few weeks ago, and I'm surprised that any of this is happening. I'm a private person, and not many people knew I was moving here. But—

"But?" the cop repeated.

I grimaced. "Sunday morning, we were having breakfast at Kali's, and I thought I saw someone out the window that looked familiar."

"Someone from a previous case?" He was writing in his notebook.

"Yes, and no. The guy I thought I saw is incarcerated and won't be released for another couple of years. But the person reminded me of him."

The more I talked about this, the sillier I felt. No matter what a freak Benjamin was, I couldn't see how it could be him.

I finished writing and handed him the pad and pen back. He radioed to his dispatch and was provided with an occurrence number. He advised the dispatcher to ensure the new one was linked to the previous one.

"That's about as much as I can do at this point. Keep vigilant and call me if anything else happens." He passed me his card. "In the meantime, I'll do some digging. It would be helpful if I could see your file on this guy that's locked up."

I nodded. "That's fine. Let me know when. I'm staying at Taylor's."

He glanced at Taylor and then back to me. "Tomorrow? I could come by Tay's house, or you could come back here."

I looked at Taylor and raised my eyebrows in question.

"What do you prefer?" he asked me.

"Your place?"

Taylor nodded.

"Fine, I'm on shift change tomorrow, going to nights, so I'll stop by on my way in if that's okay? About five?"

We settled the time, and I rose from the chair with Taylor behind me.

"Oh, just a second," he said as we faced him. "It was you that was hosed down in your hot-pink skivvies, wasn't it?"

"What?" I was confused, then it dawned on me.

"The asbestos fire?" he offered.

"Oh, uhm...how...?

"Small town." He smiled, and he wasn't being malicious. I sensed a tone of humor and realized how I responded to this would cement how I was perceived here in Oak Creek.

"You got it. What's a girl to do when exposed to asbestos? Thanks so much. See you tomorrow."

We left the interview room, and I smiled when I heard the cop chuckle.

"What was all that?" Taylor asked as he escorted me to the truck, and I noticed how he glanced around the parking lot.

"What?

"All that business about hot-pink skivvies and being hosed down."

"Oh, that. You didn't hear?" I teased. "Guess you're just out of the loop." I was trying to lighten the mood. The last couple of hours had been very intense.

He was silent when he held open the truck door and I got in. Taylor stepped back with his hands on his hips, and I thought he couldn't be more gorgeous. But the expression on his face wasn't exactly happy. His frown reached his eyes.

What had done it? The note, coming here, or the comment the cop had made? Should I try and say something funny or just let it go? I mean, if I can compartmentalize this, I hoped he could too.

"See you at home." I wiggled my fingers at him in a wave. "Toodles."

* * *

Taylor watched Drea drive off and then hurried to his truck. He wanted to follow her home to make sure she got there safely.

He was trying to figure out why he was so pissed off all of a sudden. He felt like a heel for being angry. She'd just been through something, and he was supposed to be supportive.

He left the parking lot and drove faster than he should to catch up with her.

He knew what was bugging him. It was a couple of things. First, what was all that about hot-pink skivvies? And second, she'd seemed completely different when they left the police station as to when they'd arrived. He didn't want her to be upset or worried, but he didn't want her to make light of it. This had happened before. She needed to be careful.

Hosed off in your skivvies.

Yes, he must be out of the loop, because he hadn't heard a thing about it. The threats were getting worse, and he was glad she'd reported this to the police along with the previous incidents. Whoever had targeted her was getting bolder, and that could lead to something even more sinister.

Taylor knew he was getting more and more attached to Drea. He felt it in every way. He enjoyed her presence in his home, and while she hadn't jumped in and changed everything, he liked the little touches she'd added here and there.

Taylor knew she was frustrated that her belongings hadn't arrived yet, and they'd have to figure it out when they did. He was worried she'd decide to move to her own place.

The original plan was for her to stay while she acclimatized to Oak Creek and decided where she wanted to live. But having her around, in his home—in his bed—had turned into a luxury for him. He liked it.

He also liked how their relationship was growing. Slowly, but steadily. It was an unexpected joy to have someone share his home, his life. He hadn't realized how empty he'd been until she came back to him.

Living with Drea was teaching him a little more each day and exposing to him to the fact that he couldn't suppress the past. It always came back and bit you in the ass, always there lurking in the shadows, waiting to be dealt with. That's what must be bugging him.

He saw her truck in the driveway and pulled in beside it. They both needed their vehicles to be ready to go should a call come in.

Taylor sat for a moment, mulling over his thoughts as he looked at the front door. He drew in a breath and got out of his truck. They'd been living together for three weeks now, and so far, there hadn't been any complications.

Sounds of her in the kitchen met him as he stepped onto the porch that ran along the side of the house.

He checked his watch and realized it was well past dinner time, and his stomach reminded him with a hungry growl that they hadn't eaten.

Taylor pulled open the screen door and went in.

"Hey, honey, I'm home," he called out.

Drea spun around with her hand on her chest. "My God, you scared the life out of me."

Taylor smiled and walked over to give her a kiss on the cheek. "Sorry about that. Didn't mean to. What you got going on here?"

"Throwing some hot wings into the air fryer, cutting up some celery and carrots. I'm hungry, but it's too late to do anything bigger than that. Okay with you?" she asked as she quickly scraped the skin off a carrot.

"Yep, all fine with me." He walked over to the fridge and pulled out a beer. "Want one?"

"Sure, that would be great. Nothing better than hot wings and beer."

He came over and nuzzled her neck, and she tipped her head to the side, allowing him better access to that tender spot he'd found just behind her ear.

"I can think of way better things than hot wings and beer," he murmured.

She giggled. He liked that little giggle of hers that came out of hiding when she was feeling frisky and ready for some shenanigans

"Okay, okay, all right. I'm hungry, and we can play later." She wiggled out of his grip. "I have yucky hands."

"How can I help?" Taylor asked and rested his hip on the edge of the counter. He watched her work, and it was another satisfying element to their cohabitation.

He didn't expect her to cook all the time. They usually took turns, but he sure did like seeing her being domestic in his house. Not in a chauvinistic way of course. He liked having her here as a companion, as someone in his life to share things with. He still tried to put his finger on how they were evolving in their relationship. If it was a relationship... Whatever it was, he liked it.

He picked up a piece of celery and chomped it.

"What do you think?" she asked him.

"About?"

She looked at him, frowning. "The note, the cop, everything we just did."

"Oh, yeah, that. Well—"

"You mean you forgot already? Do I have to remind you what just happened?"

Her aggravation came off in angry waves, and her tone was a complete one-eighty-degree flip from just moments earlier. It shocked him.

"Hey, what's going on?" His agitation on the drive home crept in, and he couldn't shut it down.

"What's going on?" She turned and placed a hand on her hip. "What's going on is I'm being threatened. Targeted."

"I know. That's why I urged you to go to the cops." He stepped forward and opened his eyes wide to emphasize the words. He was stunned at the way she'd jumped down his throat. He didn't understand where it was coming from.

Drea shook her head and turned back to the carrots, angrily using the peeler on them. Taylor watched her destroy the vegetable. "Look—"

She turned on him. "Look what?" she snapped. "I'm not sure you really understand. How could you? Have you been threatened like this before? Has your vehicle been keyed and tires slashed? Did anyone ever leave you a heinous image?"

She was on a roll, and he sensed that things were about to go south fast if he didn't step back and shut up. He lifted his palms up and faced her. "Okay, whoa, where did this all come from?"

She blinked and shook her head with her lips pressed together. Was she going to cry?

Taylor dropped his hands and took a step toward her. He was shocked when she subtly leaned away.

"Okay, I'm sorry for whatever it was I said that upset you. Obviously, this isn't the time to talk. I'll be outside if you need me." He wasn't sure how to handle this without it blowing way out of proportion. Maybe all she needed was a little bit of time to burn off whatever was firing her up. He'd be here when she needed him.

She returned to brutalizing the carrot, not saying anything. Taylor left and went out to the porch. What the hell was that? He ran the conversation over in his mind and shook his head.

At the station, she'd been almost upbeat after her initial meltdown in his arms. Now she was almost feral. What had happened between the police station and home?

I dropped the carrot and the peeler in the sink. What the heck just happened? Everything just blew out of proportion in a hurry.

I rested my palms on the edge of the farmhouse sink and dropped my head. Taylor was only trying to be there for me, and I was wrong to react the way I did.

Suddenly, I had no appetite. When the timer went off on the air fryer, I took the wings out and dumped them into a bowl. It had been a very emotional few hours, and I couldn't explain my behavior. Maybe everything was coming to a head. Or maybe it was something deeper. Maybe I was getting the feeling it was time to flee. To take off like I always do when I get too comfortable. Only this time, it had happened really fast. I hadn't even been here a month and was entertaining the idea of finding somewhere else to go. Usually, it took a year or so before the urge to run hit me.

My childhood had definitely fucked me up, no doubt about it. That damn fire that killed my dad had left me with fear. Fear I'd lose people I cared for. Fear of losing valuable and precious items. That's why I was anal about what was important to me.

So... I'd run when things were too comfortable. In this case, I was getting very comfortable with Taylor, so comfortable that I was living with him. Running wasn't helping anymore, though.

Should I find my own place? But that would mean making a commitment to stay here. I was being irrational, but I just couldn't get myself into a cohesive thought pattern. To my horror, I knew I was going to cry. I ran out of the kitchen and up the stairs to my room. I shut the door and flopped on the bed. Cinder was sleeping on my pillow, and he lifted his head and gave me a very quizzical look.

"I'm sorry, buddy. I didn't mean to disturb you." I reached over and stroked his neck. He stretched out his front legs, spanning his paws to show me his claws again. He started to purr and flopped over onto his back with his feet in the air.

"Animals are the best. I always feel at least a little better when you're with me."

I lay there with the cat that had adopted me and went over everything that had transpired. It was time to really think about my future. I wasn't getting any younger. I'd never really thought about hopes, dreams or where I wanted to be in five, ten... twenty years! Time ahead of me seemed infinite and unable to comprehend. Part of why I did my best to live in the moment. As much as I could anyway, but I did need reminding every now and then. Did I want to quit running and give Oak Creek a chance?

A little whisper in my mind reminded me there was still the offer from Key West.

But that meant running, moving...again. I rolled onto my side and looked out the window at the tree in the backyard. I liked it here. I liked it with Taylor.

He was a good man, and we'd found something together a few years ago. Fate had reunited us. Maybe with both of us being damaged we could find solace in each other.

A wonderful breeze blew in through the open window, lifting the curtains. They mesmerized me. I watched them dance on the gentle air and relaxed into the soft pillows. I pulled Cinder into my belly. His purring soothed me, and I was glad I'd kept him. He'd chosen me. If I hadn't found him in the wall that day... I didn't want to think about it.

"You never have to worry about being homeless again," I whispered into his soft fur.

I'd been homeless. It wasn't fun. Maybe that's another reason I was so staunch about being in control of my life. Because I did not want to be homeless ever again.

Or alone.

I had to make some changes.

Chapter Seventeen

Taylor's phone chimed. He looked at the message and puffed out a breath. Not so perfect timing. The last thing he wanted was to leave Drea without mending what had broken between them tonight.

But, he was called out to pronounce at a scene. His coverage area was large, and there were times when he had quite a distance to travel. This call was about an hour away.

He'd gone up to tell Drea, but her door was closed. He stood for a moment at the top of the stairs and debated if he should knock. It was quiet behind her door. Maybe she'd fallen asleep or was resting.

He didn't want to interrupt her, but he also wanted to clear the air on what had happened earlier. Going to bed angry was right up there with not saying goodbye when leaving. You never know what might happen.

He hated that they'd argued. It was stupid too, on both sides. Misunderstandings had the potential to do a lot of damage. But, he wasn't able to fix it right now, and would definitely make sure they did when he got back.

He kept a change of clothes in his truck and at his office.

Always prepared in case he got a call. He smiled, knowing she did the same. Between the two of them, they were always on alert. Even on a day off because something big could go down and they had a go-bag ready as well. You got used to it, but sometimes those around you, family and friends, couldn't.

Many people that didn't work shifts or who weren't on call didn't understand the demands of the job coming at all hours. It often meant people faded away over time, and it was why cops, firefighters, doctors and nurses tended to gravitate toward each other.

Taylor grabbed his keys, wallet, and identification and wrote Drea a quick note about where he was going. That done, he closed and locked the door behind him.

He'd go to the office to change and collect the coroner's van. He preferred to drive it rather than his own vehicle. He didn't like using his personal truck for security reasons and to lessen exposure to his private life.

People were unpredictable. In moments of despair and with all the emotions around a death, there were sometimes volatile situations. Look at what was happening to Drea right now.

He shook his head as he drove. It was terrible, and he felt for her. It was as if he was living it alongside her. But he was only seeing it from an outsider's point of view, not from hers. That's what led to the blow up. He hadn't done a great job at expressing his concern or simply just listening to her.

He'd have to do better.

He debated calling her, but if she was sleeping, he didn't want to wake her. She'd call if she needed him. They'd navigated their living arrangements quite well so far, and he was happy with how it was working out.

Their history had given them a head start. He liked her

in his house and in his life. Their row had jeopardized it, and he was determined to fix the misunderstanding. The drive gave him time to think about what he'd say to Drea.

Taylor pulled up to the house, the two police cruisers in front told him exactly where he needed to be. He was met at the door by the sergeant.

"I'm Dr. Peel. The coroner." Taylor introduced himself.

"In here."

Taylor followed the cop inside the house and listened as he gave background on the incident.

"It's an elderly couple. His wife is the deceased. He's taken it really hard."

He approached the location, pulled on gloves, and scanned the area. It was important to take in as much as he could without a camera. He'd make proper notes later, and pulled out his mini recorder to dictate what he saw.

Elderly woman at the bottom of the stairs. Frail, in her eighties. Possibly a fall down the stairs.

He leaned down to look closer and touched her hand.

Deceased within the past couple of hours. Blow to the head. Appears to be multiple broken bones, leg, forearm, shoulder. Head is at an awkward angle.

Taylor rested his palm on her shoulder, quietly saying a few words. It was his way of acknowledging the passing of someone. It was one of the reasons why he'd switched his medical path. He felt it was an honor to be the last witness as somebody left this world to go into the next.

Taylor stood and walked over to her husband.

"Sir, are you okay?"

Her husband of probably equal age was sitting on the step. His arms hung between his knees, and he stared blankly at the floor. Not his wife, just at the floor. I knew he wouldn't be far behind the fate of his wife. He was brokenhearted. It made Taylor sad. To love meant heartache.

There was nothing suspicious here. From what Taylor could see, she must've tripped in the upstairs hallway and fallen down the stairs. He turned to the sergeant.

"Any reason to believe this is suspicious?" Taylor asked.

The cop shook his head. "No, we've never had a call here. She was suffering from cancer and was weak. Shame to go like that."

"Any family coming to take care of him?" He looked at the husband who still hadn't moved.

"We have called some family members. They're on their way."

"Good. Because he really shouldn't be alone right now."

"Understood."

Taylor finished off what he needed to do in the house and then went out to the van. The funeral home was just arriving for the body removal.

In the truck, he sat there thinking about the old boy. Seeing his grief was a reminder of what happened when you had a life partner.

The devastation, the hollow in your heart. Was the pain worth it? Taylor found it difficult to say yes, but he was pretty sure that once the edge of grief had subsided, most would say yes, it was worth it. There was that saying about it being better to have loved and lost than not loved at all. He'd seen his brother go through the stages of grief and it nearly broke him.

Taylor hadn't loved. Yet. Sure, he'd had flings and affairs, but he'd never really gotten so close to anyone that he could call it loving. There'd been years of schooling, interning, specializing to finally become a trauma/ER doc and surgeon. With all the long hours, he'd felt a relationship would complicate things. Just as he was settling into his role, along came the patients that changed his world which led to a change in career. He knew it was out of his control. The pandemic had cause havoc worldwide. But, he'd seen the exhaustion and pain on his colleagues so he'd stepped up his shifts, wanting to relieve those with families. But, it hadn't really helped. Something he was slowly beginning to understand.

How many times had he asked himself if his sister-in-law would've survive if he'd allowed another doctor to treat her? He shook his head. Now wasn't the time to rehash it.

He shifted in his seat and thought about how sharing a home with Drea these past weeks had been like a balm to him. He saw things differently. Maybe there was room for a relationship...and if there was, he wanted it to be with her.

Just before he drove off, Taylor glanced at the house. It was neat and tidy with pretty flowers in the garden. It was obviously a well-cared for home. How many children were raised here? He could almost see grandchildren running around the house shrieking with laughter.

He thought of Drea and smiled. He could totally see a lifetime with her. Now he was eager to get home so they could talk. He didn't like leaving things as they had.

He picked up his phone to call her, and before he could dial, his phone rang. "Shit," he muttered."

"Dr. Peel," he answered. He recognized the number and knew he wouldn't be heading home anytime soon.

"Hi Dr. Peel. You're needed at another call please. There's been a multi-vehicle crash with at least three fatalities."

Taylor jotted down the location and entered it in his GPS. It was an hour in the opposite direction and away from Oak Creek. He called Drea, and her phone went to voicemail.

"Hey, babe. I left you a note that I'd been called out. I got another call now too, so I'm going to be quite late. I'll be going over to the morgue after. Looks like it will be a busy day. Let's talk when I get back. Okay? I'm sorry things went south earlier. Take care."

He was so close to saying love you. Taylor sat taller in the seat and drove off.

Love you?

Did he love her? Why would he be on the verge of saying it if he didn't? He cared for Drea deeply, but love? Slowly, a smile widened on his mouth... He was falling in love.

He gave the steering wheel a slap.

"Yup, I'm falling in love," he shouted inside the van. "Well, I'll be damned."

Taylor settled in for the drive. It was after midnight, and his dad had always said nothing good happened after midnight.

A chill rippled down his spine like a premonition. He didn't believe in that sort of thing, but he was truly unsettled for the rest of the drive to the crash scene.

Lighting and a mobile command center had been set up, turning the middle of the night into daytime. He pulled up to the command center. He'd check in and get all the info about the scene. There was likely a scribe making notes of the series of events, and they would need to know he'd arrived. This was a gruesome scene, and it would likely be a while before he was finished.

All he wanted to do was get home and pull Drea into his arms. They would be fine. He was going to make sure of it.

* * *

Something woke me up. I didn't mean to fall asleep, but I had. Maybe it was the mental exhaustion with everything that was going on and then our argument.

I shivered. It was chilly in the room from the breeze blowing in the window. Even Cinder was curled up next to me with his nose tucked in. I lay there for a moment, gathering my thoughts and wondered what time it was.

It was dark, and the house was quiet. I felt around for my phone. I mustn't have brought it when I came upstairs.

I groaned, remembering our argument. It was stupid. I'd let my emotions get the best of me and had been far too sensitive, and perhaps a tad irrational. I flicked on the bedroom light, swung my legs over the edge of the bed, and shivered again. Cinder gave a little meow.

"What? Did I disturb you? Boy, it's cold." I reached over and fluttered my fingers on the duvet. The most he could muster was reaching out his paw. He made me laugh. I loved his quirky personality. He gave another little meow and a funny yip.

"What was that? Are you talking to me?"

He stared straight at me with his beautiful liquid green eyes that were so expressive. He yawned and gave a little mewl in the middle of it.

"You're funny, cat," I told him. "But you can talk to me anytime. I'm going downstairs. Would you like something to eat?"

I got up and opened the door to the hall. The house was dark, and the only sound was the wind outside. Inside, it was quiet. Light from the streetlamp shone into Taylor's room and reflected on the polished wood floor. His door was open.

I heard a thump as my cat jumped off the bed, and then he sprinted to the landing as if he was in a race.

He bounded down the stairs at breakneck speed and barreled around the sliding into the kitchen. That cat was a treasure, and I was glad we'd found each other.

I turned on lights as I went through the house yawning. I could easily go back to bed and sleep. In fact, I think I would. I'd make a grilled cheese and a cup of tea and take it upstairs to cuddle in bed and watch TV until I fell asleep.

Cinder met me in the kitchen and rubbed against my legs, nearly tripping me. The kitchen had been renovated to appear antique with a shabby chic farmhouse/French style vibe. It had all the conveniences while still being warm, welcoming, and comfortable. A chef's dream...and mine.

I could imagine the kitchen full of family and friends and little ones at the holidays. I paused, thinking I could almost smell dinner and hear happy people in the rooms of the house. The beautiful image was almost too painful to think about. I knew deep inside that I would love to have the closeness of friends and family here. With who though? Taylor?

Our first argument was in this kitchen. I saw shadowed ghosts of Taylor and I as we argued earlier. Where was he? Did he leave? Should I be thinking of moving out? My heart tightened when my mind ran over that possibility.

I didn't want to go. I wanted to stay. With Taylor. And maybe that lovely dream of a full house could happen. But we had to fix things first. That is exactly what I was going to do when he came home.

I searched around for where I left my phone and found it over by the air fryer. The wings were covered up, and I put them in the fridge. When I turned, I saw a note on the table.

It was a short one from Taylor telling me he'd been called out. "Hmm. He didn't use many words. What did that mean? Was I overthinking? What do you think, Cinder? Am I?"

He looked up at me and wove between my legs, making little chatty noises.

I was parched. I scooped Cinder up, brought him to the sink, and put him on the counter. I know, I was spoiling him and it was unsanitary, but he was all I had right now.

I gazed out the darkened window while filling a tall glass with water. Then I remembered the fridge had a chilled water and ice dispenser. I wasn't used to that sort of thing.

I finished the water in one go and had to catch my breath. I filled it again, from the fridge this time, and checked my phone.

Two new messages. I dialed into my voicemail.

One was a callout, and the other was from Taylor. I listened to it and smiled. He felt it too. He felt that we'd had an unnecessary argument. I was sorry now, and one thing I hated was not being able to say goodbye to somebody I cared about. A hug and a kiss when they left the house was always what my mom did. I'd grown up with the same need, so I was always waving goodbye to somebody as they drove off. I hadn't been able to say goodbye to my dad. It was important to me to say goodbyes and give hugs. Because you never knew what could happen.

I couldn't do that this time though. All because of a stupid argument.

I called in to find out where I was being sent and wrote the details down in my notebook. The fire was still burning, but they knew they wanted me there. That meant it was a suspicious fire or a fatal one. I could go to the scene now and take exterior photos until I was able to get inside.

I checked the time. It was early, just coming up to three am. So much for going back to bed.

I called Taylor. It went to his voicemail, so I left one for him.

Got your message. Yes, we do need to talk. Things went a little sideways. We can figure it out when you get back. I've been called out too, and it could be a while before I get back by the sounds of it. Be safe.

I quickly made some toast with peanut butter and banana, and a cup of tea. I went upstairs to get dressed and relieved I'd had a sleep after all. This fire sounded pretty big so I packed extra clothes, a book, iPad, and threw some snacks and drinks in my bag. I was still chilled, and the tea was wonderful. I made more to take in the truck, finished my toast, tea loaded the dishwasher, and wiped down the counters.

Cinder was following me around meowing, and I realized I forgot to feed him.

"Oh, I'm sorry, baby. I didn't mean to forget you." I scooped him up to snuggle him, and he would have no part of it. He pushed his paws on my chest and straightened his legs. He wanted his food.

"Okay, down you go. Eat, and I will see you later. I won't be long." I filled his bowl and took a quick look around to make sure all was right. Nothing was left on, and the toaster was unplugged. I did this all the time. I was a double and triple checker, not trusting myself to have turned everything off that could cause a fire.

I locked the kitchen door behind me and looked back in the window to see Cinder happily diving into his bowl of food. It's a cat's life for sure.

Chapter Eighteen

I pulled up to the scene, getting as close as possible to the building without being in the way of the pumper and engine. A deep-orange glow haloed over the structure and brightened the night sky to mimic sunrise.

Flames still flickered in the windows on one side, and dark smoke rolled into the sky. It was a large building and could have served as a rooming house. Maybe it had a at one point. Now it was a tinder box that the fire crews were doing their best to knock down.

The fire chief glanced over, and I lifted my hand in greeting. He headed over, and I climbed out to meet him.

I wanted to capture images of the external structure before I went inside. If I arrived on a scene while the building was still burning and had to wait to enter, I'd take pictures of the exterior and everything that was not burning in order to rule that area out as a potential cause of the fire.

"Hey, Drea." Rage stood beside me but kept his eye on the crew and building.

"What do we have?" I asked him.

"Older structure, balloon construction. The fire made it into the wall, so it's a bit of a challenge."

I nodded. "Okay, so it will be a bit before I can get in there. Victims?"

"Unsure. One of the tenants has not been accounted for. They can't reach him by text or phone, and no one can confirm if he was inside at the time of the fire."

"Okay, I'm going to walk around and get photos from all sides while it's still working."

I picked up my camera and fell into step beside the chief to meet his lieutenant.

"That's fine. We should have it out before long. We're watching for flare-ups, rekindles, and flashovers."

I walked around to the left, to the side of the house that appeared to be untouched. Snapping away, I continued to take pictures and was able to look in through a basement window. The glass was broken, as if the panes had blown out.

Around the back, there was another window with broken glass but no shards outside. I frowned, made a nota-tion, and took some shots. Billowing dark smoke boiled out of the windows, and the flames were spread across under the eaves.

I took more photos and worked my way around the house and then back to stand beside my truck. I waited and watched the crews work, making notes. I was eager to get inside and start my investigation.

About an hour later, I was told it was okay to go in. The structure was unstable, but I wanted to get in to make sure there were no fatalities. The crews had done a primary search, but I needed to see for myself.

I could have a quick look around because I figured I'd

have to call in an excavator to knock the rest of the building down in order to find the source.

I suited up, drawing a Tyvek over my bunker gear. I made sure I had a flashlight, put on my helmet, tucked a notebook into a pocket and lastly pulled on gloves. A firefighter would accompany me into the structure.

I shivered when I looked at the building as we approached. It was spooky, like a haunted house and the hair on the back of my neck rose. I didn't want to go inside, but I had to. With a deep breath, I led the way through the front door.

After taking overall pictures, we cleared the main floor, it was full of debris. There were still a few hot spots in the wall too. Balloon construction buildings could be quite treacherous, so I was on high alert. But then I'm always on high alert. Hypervigilance comes with so much baggage.

I approached the stairs to the second floor. This was clearly a rooming house, so you never knew how many were living here. But knowing that one person was unaccounted for kept us moving deeper into the building. It was three stories, and we cleared the second floor. Again, watching for hot spots in the walls with the thermal imaging camera.

Balloon construction structures have studs that extend from the foundation to the rafters with no fire stops in between floors. They were also flanked by double brick exterior walls. If the fire got into the wall cavity, it was very hard to suppress. It seemed to run from the water to the oxygen within the walls in minutes, making it very hard to put out.

We still had to go to the third floor. I'd seen flames coming out the eaves, so I knew the fire had reached the attic space.

I pointed up the stairs, and the lieutenant nodded. He stopped me with a hand on my arm and indicated he wanted to go first. We ascended the stairs, and it did seem much more fragile than it originally appeared. The third-floor stairs were stacked on the second-level stairs, which in turn were above the basement stairs. So if one level went, they all would go.

I hugged the wall. If they gave way, hopefully, the stringers in the wall would keep their grip. The skin on the back of my neck prickled again. I had a bad feeling.

Something was wrong.

The firefighter in front carefully took each step and assessed before the next one. So far, the stairs seemed to be holding. I was getting antsy though and wanted out of the building, pronto. We had to hurry.

The walls groaned, and an eerie moaning sound in the smoke-filled darkness was chilling, then it was followed by a roar. The fire had reignited. Wood splintered behind us, and the stairs gave a tremor. I looked back in time to see the balcony hall we'd just been on collapse on itself.

Then the stairs began to fold.

I turned to see the lieutenant reach for my hand. "Book it," he shouted.

I hurried down the next two steps. The lieutenant's eyes widened behind his mask and then he was gone. I blinked and tried to reach for the wall, but I didn't get there in time, and I followed him down into the void.

Crashing through charred wood, beams, and debris, I tumbled. The firefighter's helmet light spun down, lighting up the horrific scene as it arced through the wreckage. The fall seemed to take forever, as if I were in slow motion. But the slo-mo fall came to an abrupt and very painful stop when I hit the bottom.

I tried to turn my head to locate the lieutenant and

screamed in pain. Flames filled the space above me, roaring and eating up anything in its path. It was hungry, and I was lying here useless as it bore down on me.

A high-pitched beeping seeped into my confused brain. My head hurt like a son of a bitch, and it took a second to recognize the sound as the firefighter's emergency alarm.

They'll find us now.

The fire in the structure was a living and breathing entity that did not want to be put out. It fought back against the fresh deluge of water, which in turn flowed down onto us in the basement.

I watched the dance of the flames, thinking how pretty they looked fighting the water. There was a cat and mouse game being played between them.

The beautiful, sparkly glow grew. It worried me, but I wasn't afraid. Not like I was all those years ago when a careless cigarette ignited the same kind of ravenous performance.

As it did then, the fire showed its fury to me. The walls looming above began to lean in, flames boiled over the walls and then the upstairs crumbled into the hole. We were trapped at the bottom.

I tried to curl into a ball as the flaming and charred innards of the rooming house gave up the fight against the blaze and thundered down on us.

My scream was lost in the chaos, pain crushed me, and everything went dark.

Chapter Nineteen

Just as he was finishing up the crash scene, Taylor got a message that Drea had been injured at a fire. For a moment, he couldn't breathe. He listened to the message a couple of times and then shoved the phone into his pocket. He rested a hand against the side of the van while his world tilted.

He had to get to her. He was a couple of hours away from Oak Creek now.

He took deep breaths and closed his eyes. Panic and alarm wouldn't do him or Drea any favors, but goddamn, it could be too late by the time he got to the hospital.

Forcing down the alarm and panic that began to take hold of him, he started the van and exited the crash scene. He wasn't needed anymore and would arrange for body removal. He had to get to the hospital and fast. When he realized he was rocking back and forth in the seat, he forced himself to stop and gripped the steering wheel.

He had to get to her.

His stomach soured. He grabbed the bottle in the cup holder and drank it, grimacing when the warm water filled his mouth. He finished it anyway and tossed the empty bottle in the back.

A car cut him off, and he lay on the horn.

"Outta my way, asshole!"

He zoomed around the little car and heard someone yell at him, but he ignored it. He had only one thing on his mind.

He had to get to her.

Taylor didn't try to understand the emotions he was experiencing. He couldn't right now. That would have to come later. All he could think of was getting there before...

What?

She died?

Was she in a coma?

Was she burned so badly she may not survive?

He swallowed, and his tongue stuck to the roof of his mouth. He needed more water but had none. What if he got there too late and she was already dead? What if she was too injured to pull through?

What if...

No, no, no, no. Taylor refused to consider the what-ifs. He'd learned that when he was an ER trauma doc.

Normally, he avoided the hospital. It wasn't his favorite place to be, but this time, he had no choice. Drea had listed him as her emergency contact, and that's why he'd been notified. Someone he cared about was hurt. She needed him, and he had to be there. She trusted him, inducing him to overcome his own reluctance to attend a place that held bad memories for him. But he had to help her

He had to find a way...for Drea.

Chapter Twenty

It was frustrating the message didn't give details other than she was burned and was unconscious. There was no explanation of the severity of her injuries, and damn, if his mind didn't go to the worst-case scenario.

Helplessness filled him. It was a distinct reminder of his failure from before. His hands itched, and he had the overpowering urge to be the one to care for her.

But he couldn't. Shouldn't. He'd learned that lesson once and wouldn't repeat it.

Drea would be tended by other doctors in the ER, and depending on the severity of her injuries, possibly transferred to a burn unit.

He finally came into the outskirts of Oak Creek. Morning rush-hour traffic was in full force, and the sun wasn't even up. Now more than ever, he wished he had lights and sirens so these drivers would get the fuck out of his way.

His thoughts raced over the past few weeks of them living together. Memories popped in and out of his brain like a staccato movie clip.

They'd made it work. Was it because they were continually taken in opposite directions? Both of their jobs rarely had them in the house at the same time. If they were home at the same time, one was sleeping while the other was awake.

But of course, there had been crossover, usually in the kitchen or on the stairs. On the first Saturday morning, almost a week after she'd moved in, they'd shared coffee and fresh muffins she's baked and sat on the front porch watching the day begin.

That kiss. The one on the day she'd moved in. Taylor couldn't forget it. Then their morning after the day they spent together. It had started off the shift in their relationship to one of intimacy and caring.

He slammed on the brakes when the light turned red in front of him.

"Shit!" he shouted, not caring if anyone heard.

He should've run the red. Taylor thrummed his thumbs on the steering wheel, impatiently waiting for the light to change. He stared at the green light for the crossing traffic, waiting for it to turn yellow so he was ready to go when his light changed.

"Hurry up."

Now.

He stepped on the gas, and the van lurched forward, tires squealing and the back end swinging a bit. In the corner of his eye, he saw pedestrians waiting at the corner jump in alarm. He was driving the Medical Examiner's fully marked van so he'd be waiting for complaints to pour in. He pulled his baseball hat down lower over his forehead. Weaving in and out of the cars, he made the final turn and roared up to the emergency entrance. He didn't worry about where he parked. He jumped out and ran to the door. It swished open in front of him, and he froze. Beyond those doors was where it had happened, and he hadn't been inside since. He was faced with a decision.

Most of the waiting room chairs were full. Inside were families and a variety of people on their own sitting in the emergency room. More lined up at triage, and he looked beyond the glass wall to where everything had happened.

Where he'd lost so many people. And where Drea was now. He couldn't budge, even knowing that another important person lay back there, he was rooted to the spot. He tried to move. He had to.

Taylor balled his fists and barged through the open doors, sucking a breath when they closed behind him, sealing him inside the hospital. Taking deep breaths and ignoring the welling panic that threatened to consume him, he went right to the triage desk. Of course, he was known by the staff having worked here for years prior to switching to pathology.

He saw Karen, the shift supervisor, and nodded his head at her. She looked surprised when she rounded the desk to let him in.

"Dr. Peel, what are you doing here?" She was there when it had all gone down as well. She was well aware what he'd been through and had been very supportive.

"Drea. She was brought in with burns and unconscious." Karen looked momentarily confused until he said, "The fire marshal, Drea." That was all he managed to get out. His chest tightened, and he drew in a shaky breath.

"Oh yes. But you just missed her. She was transferred by air ambulance to Mercy Memorial."

"Fuck! No one told me." Taylor could have smashed something. "How bad is she?

"Honestly, I just came on shift, and she was being taken to the pad, so I didn't have a chance to look at her chart."

"I need to go to her."

Karen placed a hand on his shoulder. "Taylor, are you okay to drive?"

He swung his gaze to Karen and saw the concern in her eyes. Yes, he needed to calm down.

Taylor nodded. "Yeah, thanks, Karen. I'm fine. This all happened so suddenly, and I was out on two calls, so I had no idea what was going on." He wasn't going to say anything more than that.

"If you leave now, you'll get there in an hour or so. But drive safely. We don't need to worry about you as well."

She gave him a hug, which surprised Taylor, but it also did him the world of good and settled him down. He hugged her back.

"Thanks, Karen. I appreciate it."

Back in the van, he headed toward Mercy Memorial. Drea had been airlifted to a level-one trauma center. Mercy was better equipped than Oak Creek Gen to handle burns and severe head injuries.

On one hand, he was glad she was getting the best care, but on the other hand, he didn't like that she needed the high-level facilities.

* * *

The drive seemed to take forever. Taylor gripped the steering wheel until his knuckles hurt. An array of emotions barreled through him, forcing him to bite back the nausea building in him He rolled down the window, and the dawn freshness blew in, helping him breathe.

He was a doctor, for crying out loud. He shouldn't be this affected. But he was, which proved to him how much Drea had grown to mean to him. He had to switch his mindset. Instead, he found himself thinking of the worst-case scenario. He would get to the hospital, and she would be dead. The sound that came out of him was foreign. It was a strange, strangled gasp.

Taylor swallowed and forced himself to snap out of it. He sourced all the calming techniques the therapist had taught him during their sessions after... Well, after.

It wouldn't do Drea any good if he crashed both physically and mentally.

So he called on all his sessions to help suppress the torment that tried to take hold of him. After a few calming breaths and squeezes of the steering wheel, he settled down and focused.

For the first time in years, he switched into his ER doc mindset. He'd let that part of him fade when he changed his career to medical examiner.

The dead don't die.

But the living do! And that's what he had to prevent now! He stepped on the gas, forcing the van to its limit. He had to get to Drea.

The drive seemed never ending, but he finally pulled into the emergency entrance parking at Mercy and parked in a spot reserved for medical staff.

This time, when he approached the doors, there was no hesitation. He sailed right through and walked up to the locked door to the nurses' station with his doctor identification in hand.

The door clicked open for him.

"I'm looking for the charge nurse, please." He glanced at the board to see if Drea's name was on it. It wasn't.

"Can I help you?" a woman in scrubs asked him.

"Yes, please. I'm looking for a patient that was air lifted in from Oak Creek. She should be here by now."

"Yes, Doctor—" The nurse glanced at his I.D. "Doctor Peel. The patient was taken straight to the ICU burn unit."

Taylor's stomach dropped. It must be bad for her to be taken there right away and not brought to the emergency room.

"Do you know her status?" He asked.

The nurse shook her head. "No, I'm sorry."

He glanced at her hospital I.D. "Thanks, Jessica."

"Take the elevators through there." She pointed past the curtained assessment rooms to the emergency exam rooms. "It's staff only."

"Thank you." Taylor rushed down the hall and punched the elevator call button.

Finally on the ICU floor, he again had to ask what room Drea was in and show his ID.

"Are you family?" the nurse there inquired.

"I... Well, sort of. We live together, and she listed me as her next of kin and emergency contact."

He'd been floored when he'd been advised of that. He was also honored that she had.

"Please, follow me." The nurse in scrubs led the way.

"How is she? Is it bad?" he asked.

"I'm sorry, I haven't read her chart. I'm not on her team, so I can't give you anything definitive. I do know she came in unconscious with burns across her back, shoulder, and arm. She's being assessed for a head injury and the severity of her burns.

This was going from bad to worse.

His mind raced the deeper they walked past the glass-walled rooms filled with an array of monitors and equipment for the patients inside. Even though being in this area of the hospital brought worry and concern to the forefront, it was also the best location for her to be based on her injuries.

She would be treated by specialists, and he'd keep an eye on her as well.

Damn, the walk to the unit seemed a million miles long.

Was this going to be another life lesson? One about opportunities missed, roads not taken, not saying how you feel.

Life is fleeting.

"She's in here."

"Thank you." Taylor stepped into the unit and watched as a medical team swarmed around a person on a bed closest to the nursing station.

It had to be Drea.

He couldn't see her yet. The wall of staff efficiently getting her settled and hooked up to monitors blocked his view.

Taylor walked over to the desk. A clerk sat at a computer screen and looked up at him.

"Can I help you?" he asked.

"Uhm, yes, is that Drea Trask?" Taylor nodded in the direction of the bed.

"Are you family?" He inquired.

Taylor explained who he was for the millionth time today, but he wasn't annoyed by it.

"As you can see, they're getting her settled, and then she'll be assessed, so we should have more answers shortly."

"Thank you," Taylor replied absently and walked over to the bed, making sure to stay clear of the team around her.

He stood back and watched them work. From what he

could see, it appeared her left arm and part of her shoulder had second-degree burns. From the treatment they were administering, it didn't look like deep tissue. He breathed a sigh of relief. Her I.V. was hooked up, and once the doctor was satisfied, he left the nurses to finish.

The doctor came to Taylor and asked, "Are you next of kin?"

Taylor glanced at his name tag. Dr. Stone.

"I am. Emergency contact. Taylor Peel. Doctor. How is she?" He peered over Dr. Stone's shoulder and then gave his attention to the man.

"Ah, good to meet you, Dr. Peel." Dr. Stone reached out, and they shook hands. "Well, she's very lucky. It could have been much worse."

Taylor shifted on his feet, frustration welling. He wanted a diagnosis. An outcome. Something. "Her prognosis?"

"She has moderate thermal burns to her left arm and lower portion of her shoulder, which we've treated with antibiotic cream."

"Her back?" Taylor asked.

"No burns. Some of her hair has burned and a small spot on her neck, but not her scalp. We had to cut her hair, which I hope she'll be okay with." The doctor smiled, and Taylor tried to return it. "I have her on an I.V. for pain and fluids. Give it twenty-four hours for us to see how the healing process has progressed. She may need I.V. antibiotic."

Taylor nodded and listened to Dr. Stone as he contin-ued, "From what I was advised, there was a collapse in the building she and another firefighter were investigating. During the fall, the left side of her Tyvek suit and bunker gear were torn open, and she was burned. She was wearing a mask, so we don't anticipate any inhalation complications, but we are monitoring."

"The firefighter?" Taylor inquired.

"Broken arm. He apparently pulled her out from under the debris, which reduced her exposure to the flames. A damn good thing, or it would have been much worse."

"Did you do a CT scan to her head? Why is she unconscious?"

"We're taking her up momentarily. It's too early to say why, but once we get the scan, we'll know more. I don't want to speculate, but I suspect it's a concussion."

"Thank God. Does she have any other injuries? Internal?" Taylor couldn't pull his eyes away from Drea. She was lying so still on the bed.

"Her thumb is broken, and she could have a hairline fracture on her right fifth metatarsal. Other than that, we'll continue to monitor her for any further injuries that may present themselves."

"Thanks, Doctor. I'll be staying with her."

Stone nodded, and the nurse came back and took Drea's vitals again. She gave Taylor a smile and a nod.

"How's she doing?" he asked the nurse.

She faced him. They probably assumed he was Drea's boyfriend. If they knew he was a doctor, it would only be a matter of time before they found out he was the medical examiner. He didn't want to play that card to ensure her treatment was the best, but he would if he had to.

The upside was the staff tended to be honest and open with him. He was thankful for that.

"She's actually doing better than I expected. We weren't sure the extent of her injuries until she arrived. She'll be going for a CT scan soon. Her burns need attention, but I've seen a lot worse. It's important they don't get infected. She will likely have scars." The nurse paused and looked at him. "Sorry, but then you know all this."

"It's fine, don't worry. I want updates as soon as you have them if you don't mind."

Taylor glanced over at Drea. Scars didn't matter to him in the least. Scars and living were better than no scars and not living. Scars were just tattoos with better stories. He did wonder if she would feel the same way and he had a feeling she would.

"I'll be here for her. Whatever treatment she needs, I will be here to make sure it happens." He didn't want to sound intimidating, but it was the truth.

The nurse smiled. "I know you will be, Dr. Peel.

She touched my shoulder as she walked out, and I turned back to Drea.

I leaned down over her so she could hear me whisper. "You'll always be beautiful to me. I just want you to wake up. Anytime now, please, just wake up."

Once they were alone, Taylor pulled a chair to the side of her bed. He let his gaze wander over her pale face. She looked small in the hospital bed hooked up to the I.V., heart monitor, finger oximeter. Her left arm was elevated and wrapped in dressing. He looked at all the machines, the IVs, catheter bag, oxygen nasal cannulas. She was covered except for her arm.

Taylor was relieved to see how extensively she was being monitored. As it should be. He was going to make sure she received nothing but the best care. Even if he had to raise hell.

She still had smudges on her face and debris in her hair. He saw where they'd cut it. It was clear they were not stylists and he smiled wryly. Another thing he had a feeling she would quickly adjust to. He didn't even want to imagine what she had gone through.

Seeing the cut and singed bits of her hair was like a punch in the gut. It was visible proof she had almost lost her life. The fear that raced through him was close to crippling. Life was fragile, and she went into situations that could take hers at a moment's notice.

Taylor rested his palm over her right hand, careful not to jar it and injure her thumb any further. He expected it would eventually be wrapped.

He leaned over, gently wiped a smudge off her cheek, and stroked her face with his knuckles.

"Come on, baby, I want you to wake up. Okay? Wake up." He hated seeing her this way. With no life in her, no sparkle in her eye or quirky grin.

He picked debris from her hair and smoothed the strands away from her face, all the while watching for the slightest change in her facial features. Taylor memorized every curve. The way her dark lashes lay against her cheek, her winged brows, and the soft way her lips pressed together.

Just the other night, those lips had left a trail of delight as she kissed her way down his chest, belly and lower. Now they were silent and still.

He'd sit here until she woke up. Taylor didn't want her to be alone when she opened her eyes for the first time. He wanted to be the first person she saw.

"Okay, babe, it's time to come back to me," he whispered in her ear.

It was incredulous he was here. How could something like this happen? She was always very aware of safety. He'd seen her in his house, always checking and rechecking to make sure there were no potential fire hazards.

She'd told him she wouldn't go into a structure until it was deemed safe. So why this time? What was it about this building that she'd allowed herself to be put in danger?

Taylor closed his eyes and dropped his head. All he heard was the beeps and whirring of the monitors surrounding Drea's bed. They grew louder and louder until the noise consumed him.

The nurse came back, interrupting his thoughts, and Taylor stood.

"We're taking her to CT now," she informed him. "This might be a good time for you to do what you need to do. I have a feeling you'll be settling in here for a while."

She smiled at him, and he nodded.

"You got that right."

A couple of orderlies and another nurse came into the room, and maneuvered around her bed to get her mobile. She still hadn't woken up, and he wondered if she would on her way to the scan, during, or on the way back.

But the nurse was right. He should make some calls to let his team know he'd be taking some time off. She would be in and out of scans, and her injuries would need attending too. So now was an opportunity for him to get some things sorted out before she woke up.

He walked out of the room and was surprised to see a number of people in the hall aside from the nurses. He glanced around, not recognizing any of them. Not that he should recognize people, but he did stumble across familiar faces every now and then from the past. He noticed one man off to the side of the nursing station. The man glanced at him and then back to his phone.

Taylor watched him for a second, thinking he looked a bit familiar, but he couldn't recall from where. He saw so many people in his line of work. The man could be anybody or nobody and right now he was a nobody to Taylor.

Turning, Taylor walked away in the opposite direction to make the necessary calls. He glanced over his shoulder and was relieved to see the man was now gone. Something about him was off.

Chapter Twenty-One

Why couldn't I open my eyes? My mouth felt funny, like it was full of wool, and something pinched my nose. I tried to reach up and move it, but my arm wouldn't move.

I heard strange sounds around me, beeping and whooshing. Distant sounds of voices. It was all so confusing, and I couldn't make any sense of what was happening. I needed to find out, but how?

And then pain swept through me from head to toe. I tried to speak. I heard my voice, and it was gibberish. What was going on? I lifted my left arm to try and feel my head, but the pain ripping through me and almost sent me back into the clouds of sleep. I tried lifting my other arm, but it was so heavy I gave up.

Prickles of panic slid through my veins. I forced my eyelids to open, but I couldn't achieve anything more than a small slit. I was in a room, and there was someone standing at the foot of my bed. I knew him.

"Taylor?" The word came out as a whisper, barely even a sound, but it caught the attention of the man standing at the end of my bed. He moved, stepping away. I couldn't turn my head far enough without searing pain in my neck. He kept looking at me, and then he was out of my line of sight.

"Don't go. T-Taylor, don't go." I was positive I was screaming the words.

He stepped back so he could see me and gave me a grin before turning, and then he was gone.

Tears welled in my eyes. Why would Taylor leave me? I didn't want him to leave me.

I moaned, and the tears of sadness turned to tears of pain. It was excruciating. My left arm and shoulder ached and burned. It was too much to bear.

I was dragged back down into the painless, black void.

* * *

The darkness weighed me down. I struggled under it and bolts of pain shot through me. What had happened to me? Where was I? If I could only open my eyes, I'd know what was going on. It hurt if I moved, so I did my best to remain still and open my eyelids.

My brain was muddled and I couldn't think straight. I was confused, but knew something was wrong. So terribly wrong.

I swiveled my eyes and the pain of moving them ripped through my skull. I let out a cry of agony, but couldn't hear anything. Was I deaf?

I blinked, slowly my vision cleared a bit and I was able to focus enough to see somebody's head on the bed next to me.

I wanted to touch the dark hair but was hesitant. Any time I moved was excruciating. It had to be Taylor next to me and I had to touch him. His head was close to my fingers and I was able to move them enough to touch his head. He was sleeping and snoring softly. So I wasn't deaf. Thank god.

He didn't wake up. And it wasn't long until I was unable to keep my eyes open, I was just so tired. I fought against giving way and sliding back down into oblivion, but I couldn't help it.

Voices permeated the layers of unconsciousness as if it were a dream. A nightmare in fact. Everything was dark except for sparks flying all around me. I cringed at the roaring in my ears, wanting to make myself small and hide. I heard sobbing. Was it me or someone else?

Something was tugging my hand. I wasn't able to move away. I was trapped in a body that refused to cooperate. The agonizing pain in my arm, shoulder, and neck blanketed me and a deep fog flowed over me, dragging me back down.

Voices again. Raised voices. People shouting and yelling pulled me back up from the depths. It was important I woke up. Something bad was happening.

I still couldn't open my eyes, and my body continued to betray me. Even my brain rejected any organized thoughts. What the hell was happening?

Then I heard a woman's voice as clear as day. "Who are you?"

I tried to say my name. I *thought* I said my name, but she repeated the question.

Then she let out a scream, and the world shook. Everything vibrated, and it brought me up to another layer of consciousness. I tried to listen to all the commotion but nothing made sense.

A voice shouted "Stop! Stop him."

What's with all the yelling? She'd asked me my name, but now she was yelling to stop someone.

Oh no, not Taylor. Why would she ask him who he was and then shout to stop him?

I fought through another layer of consciousness, but it was impossible to go any higher. I was sucked back down into the void.

* * *

It was nice here. Nice and quiet in the dark. I didn't hear voices anymore, and the strange beeping and whooshing didn't come with me in the void. I still felt funny, and the deeper I went, the less I heard.

It was nice.

It was painless.

It was peace

* * *

My body twitched. Colors were changing, and I watched as they shifted into a deep gray and then a lighter gray,

Drea, you wake up. Do you hear me? Live, live! Come back to me.

Who was calling me? I let myself sink back down into the comforting place. There was no pain. No worry. Just safety.

Wake up!

This time, it was like the word screamed inside my head. I didn't want to leave this safe place and but there was a tone in the voice calling to me and I forced myself up through the layers again. The safe darkness was getting lighter and lighter.

I know that voice.

I wanted that voice.

I couldn't think who it was. But it was so familiar. As comforting as the darkness was, the voice continued to draw me higher. The voice became sanctuary.

The voice was the new safe place.

I wanted to be with that voice.

I tried to say something, to tell the voice I was coming.

Drea, fight. Open your eyes.

The voice grew more powerful, louder and closer. I still couldn't open my eyes, but I didn't want to disappoint the voice. I fought as hard as I could to get to the voice.

Drea, I need you to come back. Fight. Fight.

I am! I fought and struggled to the brighter layers.

Fight, fight!

Doesn't the voice hear me? I just told it I'm fighting.

My eyes were so heavy, but I wanted—no, needed to open them. I had to see who the voice was.

In my ear soft, soft words. *Drea, I need you to come back. I love you.*

Finally, I was able to see through a tiny little crack. Someone must have glued my eyelids, which was dumb.

I had to see who was telling me they loved me.

"Yes! You can do it. Open your eyes. Drea come on, open your eyes. Fight!"

The voice was insistent and I wanted to tell it I was doing my best.

Slowly, the disjointed puzzle pieces of my memory began to click back together. My brain was no longer as muddled.

Fire. Falling. Pain.

Taylor. Yes, Taylor! He was the voice.

"Taylor, I love you."

He didn't say anything. Was my mouth working?

Did he hear me? Why didn't he answer me? Now I was starting to get mad. Enough of all the bullshit.

I felt his hand on my cheek, and I turned my head into his palm, even though pain seared through my neck. I moaned.

"You can do it. You can do it." He pressed his hand gently against me, and I felt lips on my forehead.

Someone was wiping my face. The warm cloth felt wonderful, and I was finally able to open my eyes.

Everything was blurry, and I saw a form looming over me. I blinked, my vision still swam and I wanted to rub my eyes back into focus.

Then I saw the face that meant so much to me. The face that trusted me to come back. I wanted to tell him not to cry when I saw tears on his cheeks. That everything would be okay.

I gazed up at him and then whispered, "Who are you?"

"What?" He looked at me and then at somebody standing on the other side of my bed.

Then back at me.

"Gotcha," I whispered, and my eyes drifted closed again. "So tired."

"Drea, don't fall asleep yet. Open your eyes."

I did as he asked and gazed up at him. "So, so tired."

"I know, honey, I know. You're going to be okay. I'm so glad you've woken up. I'm taking care of you and won't leave your side."

"I know."

"Shannon called. She wanted you to know she'd be here if she could and to tell you she loves you."

"Mmm, k," This time, I couldn't fight it. I drifted down

into sleep. I dreamt of being in his arms, of him holding me close.

I was safe.

Taylor had insisted they pull the CCTV footage of the hospital. The police got involved and supported Taylor's request.

It was important to find out who the nurse had seen in Drea's room. Not only had the guy come into her room, he'd left a note in her sheets. Taylor was pretty sure if Drea knew that, she would be unhinged.

They'd decided not to tell her about the note in the room just yet.

All it said was:

I showed you, didn't I?

The cops had the note now, and they would handle whatever needed to be done.

Taylor dropped his hand from his chin and looked at the video. Sure enough, he recognized the man who'd been standing by the nurses' station that first day.

They'd made eye contact, and Taylor was furious with himself that he'd walked away. The fact he couldn't have known this man was stalking Drea wasn't good enough. He should have been more on the ball. He shouldn't have left her.

More than ever, he wanted Drea to wake up so they could see if she recognized him.

The police inquired after the other incidents and asked if she'd kept notes. He went home for a very short while, not wanting to leave her for too long, to see if he could find anything that would help.

She kept a call log. He'd scanned down the entries and

discovered she had reached out to her previous employer to inquire about Benjamin Clark. Notations beside the date said he was still in prison. There was no way he could be here, so he'd been ruled him out as a suspect. Taylor reached for Drea's hand, scooping it gently into his.

"Who is this guy? And why is he after you?" Taylor's gaze roved over her sleeping face. She was helpless and vulnerable in this state.

What were the intentions of this guy? What had he come here to do? And why?

Taylor gritted his teeth. Had the guy really been scared off and disappeared? It was good, but also bad. It meant he could come back at any time and continue harassing Drea.

They had to find him.

He spoke to the police about putting a guard on her door while she was in hospital. They did for twenty-four hours after the intrusion. Taylor had stayed by her side too.

This was the third day in, and she was still sleeping. He'd never tire of watching her. She woke occasionally but was still very groggy from the painkillers and getting her noggin scrambled a bit.

The first time she'd woken up had been amazing. He'd finally accepted she would be okay. Even if she had been rather out of it.

He'd been shocked when the first words she'd said were to ask who he was. He'd thought she had amnesia and was about to call the doctor when she gave the tiniest smile. Relief had made his knees weak, but she was on the mend now.

He'd opened the drapes earlier, and sun rays shone in her window, falling on her face. He reached out and brushed his knuckles over her cheek. The nurses had cleaned her up, washed her face and did what they could with her hair under the circumstance. She still looked beat up, but at least she was resting and comfortable.

He dropped his head and closed his eyes for a moment. Heavy exhaustion weighed him down, he longed for his bed, only with Drea in it.

A soft moan made him sit upright.

"Drea, babe, I'm here." He leaned over her.

He saw her lips move, but there was no sound. Her head nodded slightly though. He was glad to see her respond. She still hadn't woken completely, and he was eager for the time when she would. Having her fully back, awake and alert, was what he prayed for every day.

"It's okay, babe. Go back to sleep."

Her mouth moved again, and this time he faintly heard the word, "Stay."

Taylor held her right hand, careful of her broken thumb.

"I'm not going anywhere, sweetheart."

Chapter Twenty-Two

I was now managing to stay awake for longer periods. I still wasn't quite sure what had happened to me. The last thing I remembered was walking down the stairs and reaching for the firefighter's hand.

After that, everything went dark.

Another fire marshal had been called in to investigate since I'd been hurt. I was relieved to hear the firefighter was doing okay and only had a broken arm.

They told me it was arson. Results were still coming in, but it struck me there were similarities to a case from a few years ago.

My mind was still somewhat befuddled. I knew Taylor and the officers needed me to be able to pull it all together quickly, and it frustrated me I couldn't. I was letting them down, and when I forced myself to remember, I got the worst headache.

"Hey, babe." Taylor came into my room and leaned down to give me a kiss on the cheek. The nurses told me he had hardly left my side.

I lifted my head to receive his kiss. Everything that had happened had proved to me we were good together.

"The police are coming in with some CCTV footage they would like you to look at."

My chest hurt, and my mouth dried up. "Really? I'm not sure. It worries me."

He pulled the chair from the corner to the side of my bed. "Why are you worried, sweetheart?" He took my hand and stroked the back of it.

I was a wreck with my left hand and arm burned in and my right hand having a broken thumb. Even my foot was broken. Which meant I was pretty much useless.

"I don't know. I think I'm afraid of what I might discover."

"I wouldn't be surprised if you have a bit of PTSD," Taylor suggested.

I nodded. "I was wondering the same thing myself."

"I really think you should talk to somebody to help you through this. I'm here for you all the time, you know that, but a professional could really make a difference for you."

I nodded. He was right, and I would see someone, but right now, I had to steel myself to look at the CCTV footage.

"I can't believe everything that happened while I was out of it." I stared out the window, and like a bolt of lightning, memories came rushing back. I turned to face Taylor. "I remember something. I remember voices. There were voices in my dreams. A lady screaming and commotion. Then I was being shaken."

"Even in your unconscious state, you heard the confrontation with the guy when he was in your room."

"What? A guy was in my room?" Panic nauseated me, and I reached for the cup of water and knocked it over.

"Hey there, hang on. I'll get it for you." Taylor righted the glass, poured more in, and then wiped up the puddle on the table. He held the straw to my mouth and continued talking. "The nurse came in and saw a man here. She called security to remove him, and he fought back."

"Oh my God. And I was helpless." It was terrifying to think all this had gone on while I was so vulnerable.

"There was a struggle, and your bed got knocked. That might be the shaking you felt. The doctors were worried about the IVs and your burned arm, so they had to recheck everything once they got rid of the guy."

"Do they still have him? Is he in custody?" I asked.

"Yes, they were able to hold him for a while. They hoped you would wake up and be able to identify him. He's not offering up any info."

"I guess I have to look at it then, don't I?" I sat back on the pillows, careful with my elevated left arm.

"I'm afraid so." His voice was so gentle, and I felt tears spring to my eyes.

"No tears now. You've been so brave, and this is one more step toward taking back control.

"The police can only hold him for so long, so they do want to show you the footage. Is it okay if they come in now?"

I nodded.

A short while later, my room was full of people. The doctor came in to check my arm and then left. After the doc, a nurse came in. All this happened while the detective was setting up the laptop on the bed table.

I held my breath and stared at the screen, waiting for the video. A window popped open with a movie playing. It was a video of the nurses' station where Taylor said he had seen the guy. I squinted and looked closer. It was hard to see him on the other side of the desk area. The man was sort of in a shadow, and I told them that.

"How about this then." The officer reached over, punched a couple keys on the keyboard, and a still image took up the whole screen. I gasped.

"My God. It's him." Icy fingers raced down my spine. "But it's not possible."

"Who is it?" The officer asked.

"He looks like the serial arsonist I caught a few years ago. It's hard to tell for sure, but the similarities are there." I pointed at the screen with my baby finger and then looked up at the officer. "How can that be though? He's in jail?"

"Yes, he's in our jail."

I shook my head and grimaced when my neck protested the movement. "No, no, he's in jail in Chicago."

The detective looked confused and took out his notebook "What's the name of the guy you say is in jail?"

"Benjamin Clark." I pointed at the screen. "That's him!"

"He didn't identify himself as Benjamin Clark," the detective advised me, and I was confused.

"Well, how can that be? He is almost identical to—" My mouth fell open, and I looked at the cop and then Taylor. That's it! The elusive bit of information I couldn't grasp earlier. "They're twins."

Silence filled the room and we all looked at each other.

The officer wrote in his notebook and then looked at me. "It's not something we considered, but now I think we should. If they're twins ... I'll also have someone check Benjamin Clark's status as well. If we can tie them together in some way—"

"It's not an if. I know they are twins...oh." I pressed my fingers to my temple. My head was starting to hurt.

"Okay, I think that's enough, everyone should leave,"

Taylor said. "Drea, needs rest." Taylor put his hand on my shoulder and squeezed gently.

He turned to the cop. "Do you have enough to go on? Can you come back later if needed?"

"He nodded. "Yes. You take care, Ms. Trask. We'll let you know what we find out." The officer held up his notebook and left.

I blinked and looked at Taylor, squinting against the pain. "I-I can't. I have to...!" I grimaced.

"Look at me, Drea." Taylor gently tilted my chin up with his fingers and looked into my eyes.

"See any life in there?" I asked him with a forced smile.

"Oh, yeah, lots of life. Lots of beautiful life. But you may have overdone it today."

I closed my eyes and rested my head on the pillows, not minding when Taylor fussed over me.

"Would you mind turning out the lights and closing the blinds? It hurts," I asked in a soft voice, unable to put any oomph into it.

I sighed and let myself sink into the multiple pillows I now had on my bed. I wasn't moving much with my arm still wrapped, and I hadn't been able to bring myself to watch when the nurse changed the dressing.

Taylor sat in the chair, and I looked at him. "You don't have to stay."

"I know. But I am. You sleep," he assured me.

I nodded slowly and sighed. Knowing Taylor was standing guard over me allowed me to let myself fade to black.

* * *

I felt much better today than yesterday. I was still tired with a vague headache around the eyes and the base of my skull, but I was able to stay awake longer and focus a little better.

If I kept my head in a certain position, it eased the ache. I gave up trying to hold a book. It was a no-win situation. My Bluetooth headphones were a treat though. The soft music I played helped me relax.

I must've really done a number on myself. No one had told me what had actually happened. Honestly, I hadn't been ready to know until now.

Taylor was gone. The nurse told me he'd been called out, and I was glad that he was getting back to work. I felt guilty the way he had taken time to stay by my side. But then I would have done the same for him. This incident had given me some clarity about our relationship.

The nurse, Paula, came in. She was in her fifties. She'd told me that but wouldn't narrow down an actual age. I liked her, and we had some good chats while she tended my burn. We talked almost like friends, although I was careful not to dive too deep into my past.

"It's that time again."

"Ugh, nothing personal, but I dread this."

"I know you do, but soon this will be a thing of the past. Are you going to watch today? Or should I set up the pillow wall?" She chuckled

We got along well, so when I gave her a withered look, she just laughed.

"Maybe don't bother with the pillow wall today. I'll just turn my head if I have to."

"Now that's my brave girl." She sounded proud and it warmed my heart.

I laughed this time. "I'm so much older than a girl."

I bit my lower lip and watched her unwrap the gauze.

This was definitely not as exciting as unwrapping gifts Christmas morning.

Paula glanced at me. "Okay?" I nodded and closed my eyes for a moment. "There, the bandage is off if you want to see."

Did I want to see? I couldn't understand my hesitation. Seriously, I've seen so much worse than a burned arm.

"Uhm, maybe..."

"Have you given much thought as to why this traumatized you so?" She asked.

I shook my head. Maybe I needed to figure it out. I still hadn't looked at my arm, but I took a deep breath and turned my head.

When I saw my raw flesh, I choked back a sob. It was horrible.

"It's okay, sweetie. Good for you for finally looking at it." Her voice was soft and caring.

With the wrapping removed, I felt air against my ruined skin. It was an unusual sensation. "How bad was it when I came in?"

"Worse than this. You've healed quickly and are very lucky. You'll likely only have a faint scar in a few places."

As she tended my arm, I forced myself to watch her a few more minutes until my thoughts drifted. I tried to zone out from the pain as she cleaned the skin and applied ointments. I rested my head on the pillow. An image swam just out of my reach, and I doubled down to pull it into focus.

I drew on a memory from my childhood. The fire in our house. I heard the screams and the roar of the flames and smelled the acrid smell of everything burning...including flesh.

Dad! He was on the floor by his chair, not responding to my mom or sister screaming at him. I saw his burned face, his eyes open and mouth wide as if he were wailing in pain. A melting blob of a candle was beside him and flames raced up the curtains. He'd set the place on fire!

I jolted out of the memory and startled Paula, making her jump.

"Good Lord, are you trying to frighten the life out of me?" She held her hand at the base of her throat.

"I'm sorry, but I had a memory flash back at me. Something I don't think I remembered before."

"Do you want to tell me?" She placed her hand on my knee.

"Yes, I do."

I repeated to her what I'd seen. "I was only a child when fire killed my father. We'd all been in bed when the smoke detector went off. I was terrified as Mom dragged my sister and I down the stairs. Flames filled the hall and the kitchen. It consumed the living room where Dad always watched TV."

I paused and looked at Paula. "Dad was already dead. Seeing him that way was horrifying. He'd fallen asleep in the chair with a cigarette that started it all. I think I blamed him for trying to kill us all."

Tears welled up.

"Oh, honey, you were just a child. Obviously, this is a repressed memory. Perhaps it's why you chose the line of work you're in, and why you are so diligent on fire safety?"

"How do you know I am diligent about it?" I asked and wiped my face on the edge of the sheet.

"Taylor told me. Even some of your co-workers that came to visit said you're obsessed with fire safety and are always on their asses about it. They weren't criticizing, but they did say it was a bit of overkill."

I nodded. "People have told me that before. I don't mean to be but..." I paused to think. "That must be why."

"It must be. Now let's get this arm wrapped back up."

Everything was starting to make sense now. Why I was the way I was. The reason I chose this career. My constant need to move around with no ties.

I felt like everything would always disappear, like it had when I was a kid, and I'd have to start all over again. It was as if a dark cloud or heavy weight had just been lifted off me.

I needed to speak to Taylor.

* * *

Taylor completed the scene he was called to and made his way back to the morgue for the autopsy. The family had requested the postmortem even though the death wasn't suspicious. It was unexpected, and they wanted clarity on the cause. He promised them he would do what he could and advise them.

While he prepared for the PM, he couldn't draw his thoughts from Drea. She had been his main focus for the past week. He'd spent as much time as possible with her, sleeping in the chair next to her bed and showering in her bathroom. He'd only gone home a couple of times to sleep, shower, and to take care of Cinder.

Thankfully, cats were so independent. But Cinder did express his displeasure at being left alone so much. Most of the time, he slept on Drea's bed, only coming down for food, drink, and his litter.

Taylor unwrapped the woman on the table, and his assistants came into the autopsy suite. He put thoughts of Drea away and focused on the job at hand. A few hours later, Taylor finished the report. As he'd suspected, myocardial infarction was the cause, and the family would be advised.

Taylor was excited to see Drea and eager to get back. He changed and decided to grab cheeseburgers, shakes, and fries from the pub close to the hospital. He was pretty sure hospital food was getting tiresome for her, but she'd never complained.

He'd gradually come back to work once she'd woken up and started to feel better. She encouraged him to go, and while he didn't want to leave her, he knew she was safe and healing well.

With bags of food and a tray of drinks, Taylor got off the elevator on her floor. He nodded to the nurses at the station and put a bag of fries for them on the counter.

"I hope you enjoy them," he said.

"Mmm, smells wonderful."

A chorus of thank yous made him smile as he continued past the desk. Out of the corner of his eye, a man standing next to the wall looking at his phone made Taylor pause.

"No, it's not possible," he told himself.

The man glanced at him, and he let out a sigh of relief.

It wasn't who he thought it was, and he carried on to Drea's room.

Her bed had been turned a bit so she could look out the window. When she heard him come in, her smile greeted him, lighting up the room and filling his heart.

"Hey, gorgeous." He put the bags and drinks on the rolling table and leaned down to kiss her.

"Oh, ho, gorgeous, is it? Not if you see this." She pointed at her arm with an exaggerated frown.

"Did you look at it today?" Taylor asked as he unpacked the dinner.

"Yes, and you brought me food. Outside food. Oh gimme, gimme." She lifted her good arm and wiggled her fingers.

He wheeled the table so that she could reach the food.

"Here, let me help." Taylor unwrapped her burger and flattened the paper wrapping. He dumped a pile of fries on it and squirted out a big pile of ketchup.

She picked up the cup and took a long pull on the straw, moaning with pleasure. "Mmm, chocolate, almost better than sex."

"I will ignore that remark." Taylor unwrapped his burger and sat in the chair with a groan.

"Long day?" Drea dragged a fry through the ketchup and put it in her mouth, exhibiting another sign of delight.

"Yea, I was called out and then had two PMs and reports to write."

"You're here now and can relax," she said around a mouthful of cheeseburger.

Taylor nodded and propped his feet on the end of the bed.

"This is so good." She held up the burger balanced precariously in her fingers and propped against the thumb cast. "Thanks for bringing it."

"It was my pleasure. I thought it might be a welcome change from hospital food." He grinned.

"Oh my God, you have no idea." She bit into the burger and put it down so she could grab a fry and then take a drink of her milkshake. "Have you ever mixed fries with a milkshake? It's divine."

"Can't say that I have, but I'll give it a try."

"You should. I can't wait to get home."

"Home? Our home?" Taylor asked and shoved a bunch of fries in his mouth, waiting for her reply.

She smiled and met his gaze. "Yes...our home." His heart raced. He'd hoped she would say that. "Well, it's your house, but thanks to you asking me to come and stay, it really does seem like my home too."

"I'm glad. I want you to feel that way. When can you leave the hospital?"

"I don't know yet. I guess when the doc feels comfortable about my arm." She tipped her head, indicating her left arm. "Maybe another week. Hopefully sooner. Oh, I remembered something."

"You did? From the fire?"

"Not that fire. From the fire when I was a kid. I told you a very little bit about it, but it is funny how memories can be triggered. I had this one when I saw my arm not bandaged."

As they continued to eat their meal, Taylor remained silent, listening to Drea as she recounted the fire from her childhood that destroyed her house and killed her father, and all the emotional turmoil that had stemmed from it.

He finished the burger, balled up the wrap, and put it in the bag, careful not to disturb Drea's train of thought.

He knew how important it was for her to talk about it. To get it out and unload it. When she finished and picked up her milkshake, he was shocked how much happier and relaxed she looked.

As if remembering the horrible event had woken up her soul and helped her to deal with it. As if after all these years, she'd had a breakthrough that explained all her inner fears, obsessions, and beliefs. A culmination of issues that she was finally able to make sense of.

He envied her.

Taylor knew what it was like to live with the heaviness of the past. He lived it every day. Even when he wasn't thinking about it, the load was there.

He emptied the last of his fries into his mouth and chewed, wondering if it could work for him as well? He decided the time was now.

"Drea, I need to tell you something." She raised her eyes to him.

"Okay, what's up?" He smiled watching her munch on the burger.

"It's a bit of a long story, but I feel it's time to share." He put his food down, took a long breath. "Okay, here goes."

For the next while, she remained silent as he told her about the many deaths he felt responsible for. Dr. Death, he'd referred to himself. Why couldn't he do more for the sufferers during the pandemic? Not taking the time off he should have to rest and refresh, and instead working longer hours so others could. And, how his exhaustion kept him from being on top of his game. He even told her about his sister-in-law. It nearly broke him all over again when he told Drea how he felt responsible.

When he looked up at her, she had tears in her eyes. His heart swelled. She was crying for him. He took the hand she reached out to him.

"Come here," she said, her voice soft.

He did, and sat on the bed. She pulled him down until he was lying beside her, careful not to hurt her.

"Shh, I'm okay. You won't hurt me. Let me take some of your pain away," she said quietly. "And, you were not to blame."

He draped his arm over her belly and did his best to relax, ever careful not to put too much weight on her.

They lay in silence, neither saying a word. He'd told her something so painful, and she'd taken it in. Never had he felt so at peace.

Chapter Twenty-Three

A week later, I was tucked up on the couch in front of the window looking across the front lawn of Taylor's house.

I was discharged after I gave some push back to leave. They wanted to keep me for another few days to ensure that my burn was getting the proper attention, but Taylor had stepped up and said she was going home with a doctor. He could handle it.

It was one of the first times I'd heard Taylor announce to the world that he was a doctor and not a medical examiner.

Even after the tragic telling of his Dr. Death feelings, I trusted him. I told him so and we'd clung to each other in the hospital when he'd finished. There were no words of comfort I could offer him, only the silence of listening and being there for him. There had been a big shift in our relationship after that. I felt it, and he told me he did too. We were closer than ever.

Cinder was curled up on my lap, and I stroked him. He

purred like a motor, and his eyes were half closed as he basked in the sun that came through the window.

I was pretty sure he'd missed me. Of course, he'd given me the silent treatment when I first got home, but it wasn't long before he forgave me.

It was still difficult for me to do anything, even the simplest task was tough. Taylor had set up a table beside me with everything I could possibly need while he was gone. Even an ice bucket to keep drinks chilled so I didn't have to get up. I had the remote control for the TV. I had my laptop. I had my phone and even a couple of books to read. I was set.

The comforter made me feel cozy, and the soft pillows behind my back were so much better than the hospital bed.

I had to remind Taylor I wasn't an invalid, and that it was okay for him to go to work. Should anything happen, I would call. The last I'd heard the bad guy was in police custody.

It was just so damn good to be home.

* * *

The house was quiet and my headphones played calming music softly. I let out a sigh as I woke up from yet another nap and a wave of feeling useless washed over me. I was unable to really do anything, physical or mental. I was exhausted. The doctors had advised me to expect this and said I'd bounce back. But I wasn't bouncing as quickly as I wanted to.

I rested back on pillows and turned my face to the ray of sun coming in the window. Warmth spread over me, and the scent of flowers from the garden came in on the breeze.

I was looking forward to Taylor coming back from work.

He was going to bring pizza, wings, and some beer. We were going to talk. Talk about us, where we are, and where we're going. We still hadn't discussed our unfortunate argument just before my accident, but I wasn't sure we needed to. It was as if we both understood where it had come from, and everything was fine.

We'd grown closer, and I really wanted to figure out if we could make it as a couple.

My thoughts drifted off into nothingness, and I stroked Cinder's soft neck. His purring lulled me, and I drifted off into a shallow nap.

Cinder jumped off me, his paws digging deep into my belly, and it woke me up with a start.

"Damn, why do you do that? It hurts, you know." I reprimanded him as he ran into the kitchen and knew full well he didn't care in the least. I took off the headphones and listened to the birds singing outside.

I had to go to the washroom, so I got off the couch and steadied myself. I saw the walking stick that Taylor had left right beside the coffee table. I felt a little unsteady and used it to shuffle my way to the washroom. The window was slightly open, but the blinds kept it private.

Sounds of birds tweeting came in the window, and there was a thump that must've been Cinder jumping off the counter. He was probably looking for food.

I couldn't see him. I looked out the window of the kitchen door to see if he'd gotten out, opened it and called him. He came from the laundry room, taking his own sweet time.

"There you are, you rascal."

A funny smell made me wrinkle my nose. It was a weird citrusy or lemony odor with a tinge of something else I couldn't quite place. Someone could be painting or varnishing.

I closed the door and locked it. Picking a few treats for Cinder from the jar, I tossed them on the floor. He chased after them quite happily, and I made my way back to the couch. That was enough exertion for now.

Once comfortable, I took a bottle of sparkling water from the ice bucket. Taylor had cut up some lemon—he was so thoughtful—and I dropped a couple of pieces in the glass.

This past week, he'd really shown his caring side, and I reveled in the love I felt for him.

I put the drink down and then leaned back into the pillows again when I heard a ping on my laptop. An email had come in. I struggled to a sitting position and balanced the laptop on my knees.

I was expecting a copy of the fire report on the building that had collapsed. I'd also asked for a report on the abandoned house that had caught fire a few weeks ago.

I scrolled down to find what I was looking for. The cause of the fire. It was like I'd been smacked up the side of the head.

"Of course," I whispered to myself. "Why didn't I remember this?" I switched to the other analysis report and scrolled down. The same cause.

My laptop and belongings had arrived while I was in the hospital. I opened the folder and scanned until I found the notes I'd made on Benjamin Clark.

"Holy shit." I looked out the window as everything started to click into place.

It's the connection we were looking for. I grabbed my phone and called Taylor. He answered quickly.

"D, is everything okay?" I heard alarm in his voice, and I assured him I was fine.

"But listen, I can't believe it, but I found the link. I found the link between all the fires."

I was so excited that my heart was racing, and I could barely catch my breath.

"Okay, you sound like you are having a bit of a panic attack, are you okay? Breathe deeply."

"I'm fine. Really fine. Linseed oil."

"Linseed oil? What do you mean?"

"Rags soaked in linseed oil covered in a cardboard box or even in under a pile of cardboard will eventually ignite. I just got the report that the rooming-house fire was also started with linseed oil rags. It proves the connection."

"Listen, I'm on my way home. I've got the food, so we can go over the reports when I get there. Call the detective and get yourself settled down. Sound good?"

"Yeah, sounds good. Did you ever hear back from the police about the guy that came into my room? I don't remember how that was resolved," I asked. Silence. "Taylor?"

He cleared his throat, and I knew I wasn't going to like what he was about to tell me.

"They didn't have enough evidence to hold him, so they let him go. He was charged with something and released with a warning to not leave Oak Creek and some other conditions."

I was silent. I didn't know what to say. He was back out there. Suddenly all the safe feelings I had vanished. I was vulnerable again and this time I wasn't mobile enough to save myself.

"Listen, D, I'm not far from home, not even five minutes away. Let's chat when I get there, okay?"

"Okay." My voice came out as a squawk. "Please hurry."

I put the phone down, glad I was back on the couch

because I felt like I was falling and totally off-balance. Cinder hopped on the arm of the couch, startling me. Icy fingers of dread tingled along my spine.

I was afraid. All over again.

Was the house secure? I'd locked the kitchen door, but I hadn't checked the others. Taylor would have done it earlier in the day. I was frozen to the spot and couldn't bring myself to get up and check.

Taylor said he was close to home. So, I would wait for him. Here, on the couch by the window.

A sour taste filled my mouth, and I reached for the mug of sparkling lemon water. I finished it with a grimace when the bubbles stuck in my throat like a stone.

I had an overpowering urge to hide.

Taylor said he wasn't five minutes away. So I stayed put on the couch and watched out the window for him. My phone ready to dial 9-1-1 should I need to.

This guy was an arsonist and could start a fire multiple ways. He didn't need to be in a building to do it. Oh God, what if he set something here?

I needed to check the house. As if the couch was clutching me tightly, I couldn't seem to get off it.

I heard Taylor's truck engine down the street and closed my eyes, saying silent thank you as he pulled into the driveway.

He burst through the front door, startling Cinder, who took off like a shot.

"Oh, Taylor," I cried. He sat beside me, pulling me into the security of his arms. "Why would they let him go?"

"I don't know, honey. But it will all be okay." He crooned in my ear, holding me tightly, and I began to relax into him.

My arm hurt, and I had to shift out of his hug to look at

him. "I'm worried he knows I live here with you and will do something."

"He wouldn't dare." A fierce expression on his face.

I nodded. "Yes, he would. We have to check the house."

Taylor helped me up.

"What would we look for?" he asked while gazing around the room.

"My suspicion is he'll use what works for him." I picked up the walking stick.

"Linseed oil," Taylor said.

"Yes. We need to look for a pile of rags. They could be in a box shoved in a corner or under something. It could be pretty much anywhere. After a few hours, the rags will spontaneously combust. I think we should hurry and check. Time is running out.

"I'll take the basement, and you look here, then we can go upstairs." Taylor took control, and I was happy to let him.

"I was sleeping most of the day. He couldn't have come inside, could he?" Alarm rang in my voice. I took a deep breath and stepped toward Taylor. "The kitchen door was unlocked. What if he came in and I had no idea. He could have started a fire while I was sleeping."

He placed his hands on my shoulders. "Shh, calm down, honey. Let's focus on finding those rags. I'm going to call this in as well. Just in case."

I nodded, swallowed, and gripped the walking stick firmer.

"O-okay, what you said is a good idea. You go check, and I'll look around here."

I didn't think there would be anything concerning on the main floor, but I still looked under the kitchen sink, in the broom closet, and laundry room. I was about to go to the pantry when I smelled smoke. I spun around, screaming for Taylor at the same time.

He came bounding up the stairs before I even got to the kitchen door leading to the wraparound porch.

"Smoke. I'll get the hose," I instructed him. And just like that, my fear, lack of confidence, and fragility vanished. I was me again. I had a purpose, and even with a bum arm and a broken thumb and foot, I had to handle this, or we could have a big fire on our hands.

We raced outside, well, I hobbled, and didn't have to look far for the origin of the smoke. It was starting to billow from a stack of wood leaning against the wall of the house.

"Douse it!" I yelled just as the first flame popped up through the logs.

I heard sirens from fire engines as we did our best to knock the logs away from the house and hose down the developing fire.

"Stay back, Drea. I don't want you getting burned again. Your bandage could ignite. Please just get back," Taylor told me, and I knew he was right.

The adrenaline rush was starting to fade, and I'd never been gladder to hear sirens and the screech of tires as the firetrucks and police cars pulled up to the house.

Taylor was losing control of the building flames, and I feared the worst. They were licking up the wall and starting to fan under the porch roof. It was like a tinderbox and could go up quickly.

Then a stream of water struck the roof and wall. A firefighter shouted for Taylor to stand aside, but a little too late, and he was hit by the spray.

He fell over and pushed himself to his feet. He came to stand by me and watch while they knocked down the fire.

"Are you okay?" I asked him. "I know how water from the hose can hurt when it hits you."

He glanced at me, looking puzzled, then back at the crew as they quickly got the fire out.

The lieutenant walked over as he spoke into his radio. "Hey, Tay," he said reaching to shake his hand. "What the hell?" He hitched his thumb behind him at the fire scene. "Grilling mishap?"

"Yeah, yeah, Josh. Smart ass. This is where I turn you over to Drea. She's the one that can fill you in."

Josh turned to Drea. "So what happened here? How can you fill me in?"

I didn't like his tone. At all. But then maybe I was just being super sensitive.

I pointed to the burned area. "Fire." I stared him down. He was the first to look away, and I heard Taylor give a light cough.

"It's arson. The accelerant—"

"Wait, just hang on a minute. How do you know it's arson?" Josh looked skeptical.

"Because I know. It started with a pile of linseed-oil-soaked rags." I hobbled toward the porch and squinted through the remaining smoke.

"Hey, don't get too close. You might hurt yourself." Josh reached out and grabbed my bad arm.

I let out a yelp and turned on him. "Listen, I know how to handle myself around fire scenes. I'm an investigating fire marshal." I snapped at him.

The shocked look on Josh's face was pure pleasure. He'd been a dick since he'd arrived on the scene, and it was nice to put him in his place.

"Oh, ah. Okay, then. My apologies," he said.

I nodded. "It's a big, long drama, but the guy who set this

fire is the twin brother of another arsonist incarcerated in Chicago. I suggest you let one of the cops know, since they just released this guy, and here he is at it again not hours after being released."

Josh pressed his lips together and turned to face the officer on scene.

I reached for Taylor, and he was instantly by my side.

"Did he hurt your arm?" he whispered to me.

"I don't know, maybe, no, not really. It stings. I'm exhausted again." I leaned into him, and he helped me back into the house. "This is so frustrating! I can't believe how weak I still am."

"You will be for a while. Your body took a beating, not to mention your noggin." He gently tapped my head.

"Well, so much for our foodie night," I said and settled on the couch as he draped the comforter over me.

"Listen, I'll take care of everything outside. I'll put the pizza & wings on the table, and here's a Dr. Pepper. Everything's all within reach. You rest."

I tugged on Taylor's hand. He bent over, and this time, he kissed me on the mouth.

"Mmm, it's been way too long," I murmured against his lips.

"Yes, it has been." He deepened the kiss. Oh, how I wanted this man.

"I was thinking, sponge bath later?" He winked.

"Sounds wonderful." Cinder jumped on my thighs and promptly curled into a ball.

I lounged back into the pillows and listened to the voices outside. I had every confidence in the fire crew, even with dickhead Josh. But he had apologized so I'd give him that. I knew they would make sure everything was okay before they left.

Now the police just had to find and arrest the twin

* * *

"What a day." I snuggled into Taylor, careful of my healing arm.

"It definitely was. It was very cool to see you in the groove, so to speak. Doing your job."

"It was strange. Because this is your house. This is the house that I'm living in with you. I've brought all this drama into your world, into your home." I looked up at him and gently touched his cheek, turning so he would look at me. "I'm so sorry."

He gazed down, and the feeling reflected in his eyes was all I needed to see.

"It wasn't your fault. You are only doing your job, and it goes to show you some people are really sick. I'm just glad they know who they're looking for. The proof that you discovered by cross-checking your files with the causes of other fires was exactly what they needed to connect him and to his brother. Both had a vendetta against you and played it out. Now they just have to find him."

I shook my head. I really thought that once I closed the Clark case and he was incarcerated, it would be over. How very naïve of me.

My phone rang and I grabbed it. I knew it wouldn't be a call out, but I hoped it would be news on the other brother. I pressed speaker so Taylor could hear as well.

"Hello?"

"Is this Andrea?" A male voice inquired.

A trickle of alarm skittered down my spine and I glanced at Taylor before answering. "I-it is." I held my breath waiting and praying it wasn't the twin idiotic brother to threaten me again.

"Yes, this is Sgt. Walker, your stalker case was referred to me. I'm calling with some new information."

I sat up and grimaced when I knocked my arm on the chair. "You do? Please, tell me."

"As an investigator yourself, you're probably aware that suspects can linger at the crime scenes to watch their handiwork."

I held my breath. "Yes, I'm aware."

One of our officers on the scene at your house today noticed a person in the crowd that matched the description of your suspect. I wanted you to know, we took him in for questioning, and he was indeed, responsible for the notes and arson at your house. He has been arrested and now in custody."

Relief washed over me and I dropped the phone and took Taylor's hand. I was at a loss for words so he spoke for me. "Sgt. Walker, this is Taylor Peel, Andrea is processing this information and I can tell by the expression on her face, she is relieved, and a bit overcome by this excellent news."

"Ah, yes, Dr. Peel. Thanks for relaying. We will need an officer to come around and take a full report to add to the one we've already generated. Also, we'd like her to confirm identity when she's up to it."

I shook my head. "No, I don't want to see him in person. Just a photo if I have to." I whispered to Taylor.

"Uh, well, the identify confirmation part could be a bit of a problem. Perhaps it can be by photo? But the officer coming is fine." He looked at me and I nodded.

I cleared my throat. "Yes, the officer is fine, please just let us know when."

"Will do, and the officer will have a photo for you to

view. In the meantime if you have any further questions don't hesitate to call me."

Taylor put the phone down and I rested against the nest of pillows.

"It's over," I whispered, and when the tears welled up in my eyes I didn't even try to hold them back.

"Oh, baby. It's all fine now." Taylor gathered me into his arms and I wept.

All the years of hypervigilance, trauma, death and despair came crashing down around me. For the first time I could remember, I felt safe. And I wasn't alone.

I had Taylor. And he had me.

"I don't like to see you upset like this. But, let it out. You've bottled it up for far too long and I'm here for you, always," he murmured against my hair.

His words, and the relief coursing through me was too much and all the pent up memories and anguish came out full force. I cried in his arms for what seem liked forever,

"Oh, Taylor. I'm so glad we found each other again."

"Me too, honey."

Later that night, after his promised sponge bath, we lay naked on my bed. I still wasn't able to use the shower, concerned about bathing in case I slipped, fell, cracked my head open, or broke something else. But, I couldn't be happier being attended to by this man of mine.

My head rested on his shoulder and his arm was around me, careful to avoid my bandages and his other hand resting on my belly. I shivered a little and he pulled the comforter over us.

"You're healing well," he said and gave me a little squeeze.

"I'm glad to hear you say that, Doctor. I hope that there isn't too much scarring." I tried not to sound down about the possibility of burn scars and looked at the positive. I was alive and healthy. It could have easily gone the other way.

"It doesn't matter to me if there are scars. It's just part of who you are. And speaking of that," he whispered, rising on his elbow. "There's something I've wanted to say to you for a while."

I gazed up at him, and an overpowering emotion swept through me. I finally accepted I was so in love with him I couldn't imagine life without him. It hadn't taken long for our feelings to emerge and overpower us. Danger does that to you I guess. I held my breath, waiting to see what he was about to say.

"Drea, when we met all those years ago, I had never met anybody as vibrant and full of life as you. I know we made the pact that weekend that it was a one-off, but I wasn't able to get you out of my mind. I thought about you constantly, and I wanted to try and find you."

"I know. It was the same with me. Once I got home, I couldn't believe the emptiness that I felt not being around you. But I also remembered what we said to each other, and I honored our agreement. Much to my detriment, of course." I smiled at him and turned my head for a kiss.

He slipped his hand around my neck and up into my now shorter hair style. The kiss deepened, and I knew where it would lead us. We hadn't made love since before my accident. And oh, how I wanted him.

"I will admit that I did try to find you. Without knowing your last name, I called a couple of places, but you had left. So I took that to mean that it wasn't meant to be. But, when I saw you at the fatal fire all those weeks ago now, I realized just how profoundly you touched my life. We'd been brought back together, and I suppose the universe had other plans for us."

"It did." We gazed into each other's eyes. "I'm glad the universe took matters into its own hands."

"Me too. See, meant to be," he said.

"Yes, meant to be." I paused and felt tears prickle behind my eyes I was so overwhelmed with emotions. "I love you, Taylor."

"I love you more." He smiled at me and I melted.

We laughed at the time when our words overlapped each other.

"I suppose I could say double jinx. Having said the same thing at the same time as you."

"No jinx here," I assured him.

He leaned down and pressed his lips to my neck, gently kissing me up to my ear and over to the side of my mouth.

"No, no jinx here." I turned my face, and our lips met. We came together with the passion of love and knowing we would be able to overcome our past and build an amazing future, together.

Thank you for reading Backdraft! I hope you enjoyed meeting Drea and Taylor. Second chance romances can be so sweet once they overcome the obstacles in their way. I'm sure you'd enjoy AFTER THE HURT for some steamy hotness. Find out if Tank will forgive Pepper for running away at the worst possible time..

CLICK HERE TO READ AFTER THE HURT NOW >

And if you enjoy reading hot stuff, you'll love the sexy, and daring GET IT ON COLLECTION. Available as an omnibus, and separate quickie novellas.

"Five S's to describe these stories: Sultry, Sensual, Saucy, Sexy and Steamy!"

• Goodreads reviewer

Authors appreciate your help in spreading the word to other readers, including telling a friend. Reviews help readers find books, so please leave a review on your favourite book site.

You can join by Facebook reader group, Shana's Shananigators, for fun, exclusive sneak peeks of upcoming books and giveaways.

SIGN UP FOR SHANA GRAY'S NEWSLETTER HERE >

After the Hurt Teaser

Tank stared into her violet eyes. The ones that had the ability to turn him inside out. But not today. Not tomorrow. Not ever again.

But, those damn shoes. They matched her flaming red hair, and the memory of her sprawled naked before him, arms flung wide, was imprinted on his brain forever.

Like it was yesterday, he could still see her alabaster skin in vivid contrast against the glossy black sheets. The clear violet of her eyes, gazing at him under her finely arched ginger brows.

She'd lain there, taunting him to do as he wanted with her. And he had.

After the Hurt Blurb

Pepper Chapman refuses to throw in the towel. Nine months ago, she made the biggest mistake of her life. Blinded by grief after her mom's death, Pepper abandoned the man she loves. Now she wants a second chance at everything she gave up: strong hands driving her to ecstasy . . . a deep voice whispering naughty promises in her ear . . . the future they'd planned since they were teenagers... and his love. So Pepper comes home looking for forgiveness, ready for a new beginning—if he's willing to give her a shot.

Retired MMA star Tank Sherman may be used to low blows, but Pepper's emotional sucker punch left him reeling. Trying to ignore the pain and forget the pleasure of her body beneath his, Tank is prepared to ring the final bell on their relationship. Then Pepper shows up out of the blue, radiating a sensuality he's tried hard to forget and anting his forgiveness. But Tank won't let himself get hurt again, and that means resisting the heat that still burns between them. Because if he takes Pepper back, he knows he'll never be able to let her go again.

Originally published with Random House, Loveswept.

About the Author

 **Shana Gray** writes contemporary romance and women's fiction with heat and she's always eyeing the next story line. She lives in a small town in Ontario, Canada, is a mom of two grown sons, a wonderful daughter-in-law and in love with her new grandbabies. She's human to her rescued Golden Retriever, Hiro. When she's not writing, she can be found daydreaming about life, feeding her crow friends, in the garden and making travel plans to far off lands to feed her wanderlust.